LINDA MARSH

By ADÈLE DE LEEUW

A PLACE FOR HERSELF

RIKA: A VACATION IN JAVA

ISLAND ADVENTURE

YEAR OF PROMISE

ANIM RUNS AWAY

DINA AND BETSY
(Picture books for younger children)

DOLL COTTAGE

CAREER FOR JENNIFER

GAY DESIGN

LINDA MARSH

LINDA MARSH

by

Adèle de Leeuw

THE MACMILLAN COMPANY

New York, 1946

LINDA MARSH

CHAPTER ONE

LINDA stood in the doorway and looked at her new bedroom with pride. It was much bigger than the one she had had to share with Amy in Wayneville, and this one was hers—entirely hers! A bed, one chair, and a small chest of drawers was all that it contained at the moment, but Linda was busy furnishing it in her mind's eye for the hundredth time. It was going to be so hard to decide what to have ... long frilly curtains and peach walls and a blue chenille spread, or chintz draperies and bedspread and a skirted vanity table? And should she buy a maple desk to match the chest, or would it be more fun to have all painted furniture and a figured wallpaper? Of course the budget would have something to do with it. But within the amount her father had said she might spend, there were so many possibilities. And this was only one of the rooms to be done!

"Miss Linda!"

It was Mrs. Parsons, the housekeeper. Linda sighed. There would be something wrong, of that she was sure. She had expected to call the maid Florence; but Mrs. Parsons had said firmly, in the very beginning, "I'm a housekeeper. And my name is Mrs. Parsons." She was large and imposing, and Linda sometimes felt inadequate before her penetrating glance and accusing tone. She knew she was lucky to have got anyone at all in these times, and Mrs. Parsons *was* a good cook and cleaner; but she wished the housekeeper would occasionally relax. It was hard to live up to her.

"Miss Linda," Mrs. Parsons said in a voice that boded ill, "I've stood all I can stand. I made up my mind to speak to you about it, and I think you should do something about it."

"Oh dear, I hope she isn't going to leave!" Linda thought miserably.

Her father would be annoyed—he had had a hard time getting Mrs. Parsons, and he would feel that she ought to have been able to manage a servant and keep the house running smoothly.

"What is it—now?" Linda asked.

She couldn't resist tacking on that "now," although she knew at once by Mrs. Parsons' expression that it was the wrong thing to do.

"I'm sure I'm a patient woman, Miss Linda, and I don't say half of what bothers me. But this has got to stop. I need my rest. When I work all day I've got to sleep at night, and the noise and them fumes is more than a body can put up with."

"Noise? Fumes?" Linda was mystified.

"It's Master Bob." Mrs. Parsons was thin-lipped.

Bob was Linda's younger brother, a lively, towheaded,

8

intelligent, and inquisitive boy who, with whoops of joy, had appropriated as his one of the rooms on the third floor across from Mrs. Parsons'. Linda began to have some inkling of what was coming.

"He's up at all hours, playing that radio. Foreign stations they are, talking queer languages that you keep listening to and can't make head or tail of." Linda wanted to smile, but thought better of it. "I lie awake listening, thinking I'll hear something, and I can't make out a word. And all that static and loud noise keeps me from sleeping. And when he isn't doing that, he's making experiments!" She puffed out her cheeks and bit off the word in syllables so that it sounded like something dreadful. "Ex-per-i-ments with that chemistry set of his. Terrible smells and smoke and fumes all the time. I'd like to have choked the other night. It got in my bronchial tubes and set me to coughing so I was all upset for hours on end!"

"I'll speak to him, Mrs. Parsons," Linda promised. It would be awful to have Mrs. Parsons leave because sulphuric acid had disturbed her night's rest. "Bob is so wrapped up in his chemistry, you know—"

"All well and good, and boys will be boys; but some smells I can't stand, and nighttime is no time to go experimenting with heathenish odors."

"Of course not. I'll talk to him when he comes in. Did he say where he was going?"

"Not to me, he didn't. And I'm not one to keep track of the whole household's coming and going. I've got my hands full as it is."

9

Linda felt baffled. She knew she ought to say something to Mrs. Parsons, something definite and firm, but she did not know what it was nor how to say it. Instead she turned back into her bedroom, indicating that the interview was over; and after a moment she heard Mrs. Parsons clumping down the hall toward the back stairs. "Now," thought Linda unhappily, "she'll be cross again and probably scorch the potatoes." Oh dear! She had dreamed of the time when they could afford a housekeeper—someone to take the heavy chores off her own shoulders—and now that time was here, but somehow it wasn't as she had imagined it.

There seemed to be just as many things to look after, just as many situations to cope with, just as many difficulties to solve, as before. Even more. When they had lived in half of the two-family house in Wayneville, and she had looked after the household, ordered and cooked the meals, bought the clothes for Bob and Amy and herself, and organized the household duties for all of them, it had been comparatively simple. There had been a woman to come in twice a week to clean and do the laundry, but the rest had devolved on her and the two younger children. When they had all had duties to do they had done them—grumbling sometimes, but never openly rebellious. They had realized, perhaps, that they were all part of a close-knit group, in which each one must do his share. It had grown naturally out of their desire to help their mother, when she was ill those long three years. And after her death—even now Linda felt a

stab at her heart like a physical pain and squeezed her
eyes tight shut to keep the tears from falling—after
their mother's merciful release into death they had gathered round their father and promised to keep the little
family intact.

"We'll all help." She could hear herself saying it, that
drab, dreadful day when they were so alone, so bereft.
"If Amy and Bob help, I know I can manage, Daddy."

She remembered her father's worn face, ravaged with
grief; and the way he had looked at her—as if she had
offered him a light in a dark room—had given a lift to her
spirits.

"I know I can count on you, Lin," he had said. "On all
of you."

It hadn't been easy. It hadn't been easy, either, all
those years of her mother's illness. Carrying her school-
work and the increased burden of the work her mother
wasn't able to do. Trying to save during those hard years
when her father had had no work at all, and then only a
job that he had taken to tide them over. Washing the
windows to save the cost of having a man in to do it.
Learning the cheap cuts of meat, ways to do without meat
at all. Making over her dresses with her mother's super-
vision. Taking the children to school and calling for them,
because they had sold the car and there was no bus that
passed their way.

It had been a busy life, giving her little time of her own.
She'd managed to keep up with her classes at school, and
that was all. There wasn't time for the parties and outings

her classmates enjoyed, because she had to hurry right home from school—always. To relieve her mother of chores, to relieve the part-time nurse they had to get in later on, to take care of the children, to cook dinner for all of them.

She wasn't sorry to leave Wayneville when the time came. It had been a place of unhappy experiences; of struggle, and their beloved mother's death.

When her father came home one evening, full of repressed excitement, and said, "Well, chickens, how'd you like to move?" they had all shouted, "Where?" They had added, "Why?" and "When?" and their father had laughed.

"Looks like it's unanimous. But one question at a time. First—where. I'd thought of New Jersey."

"New Jersey!" they shrieked. "But why?"

"Well, that's the second question. Because, my little rapscallions, I've got a new job. In New York City."

Linda, watching her father, knew that it was wonderful news. His eyes sparkled, and the lines in his face creased with happiness. And whenever he called them extravagant, ridiculous names like that, he was feeling on top of the world. It had been a long time since he'd called them "rapscallions."

"As what, Daddy? Tell us, for goodness' sake! We're all dying of curiosity."

"It came out of the blue." He leaned back in his chair and lit his pipe. They had to wait, grouped around in impatient attitudes, while he filled the bowl and lit the match

12

and nursed the flame. "I'd have given my eyeteeth to get with the Hobart Engineering Company some years ago, but there was never an opening. Always a promise to keep me in mind, of course, but that's as far as it went and I didn't put any store by it. But last month came a letter from the president, asking if I'd like to join their office as electrical engineer—"

"Daddy! And you never said a word!"

He smiled. "Keep a secret pretty well, don't I? Fact is, I was afraid to mention it for fear the charm would break. I didn't want to raise any false hopes in you—or in myself, I guess. . . . Well"—he puffed contentedly a moment —"of course I said it sounded good to me, and today Mr. Hobart himself stopped off in town and had a talk with me. It's all settled now but a few details. So I thought it was time for a family celebration."

"Oh, Daddy, it's wonderful!"

"Can we have a dog?" Amy demanded.

"Will it be near the water? I've got to try out my new boat," Bob said. His eyes shone. "Of course there are lots of kids I'll hate to leave, but I'm sort of tired of this burg. Where are we going to live?"

Mr. Marsh laughed. "You're rushing me. All I know is that I'd thought of New Jersey. I'm going down to New York for a conference next week and I'll take some extra days and see about a place to live. We may have to take what we can get for a while." He sat up straighter. "But one thing I'm determined about. We're going to have a place where we can stretch . . . a house all to ourselves,

13

with a bit of garden so I can putter around on Sundays. I want to live in a town where there are good schools and churches and plenty of trees."

"And a lake, or a river, maybe?" Bob said.

"And where we can have a dog," Amy insisted.

"Yes, with water, and a yard big enough to hold a dog," their father conceded fondly. He held out his hand to Linda and she came forward and took it. He drew her close. "And what's your particular specification, Lin?" he asked. "You've been so quiet since that first outburst. Isn't there something special you want?"

"Well," she said slowly, "a room of my own would be nice—"

Amy snorted. "That goes for me, too! I want a closet all to myself, and if I feel like reading in bed I don't want to have you saying, 'Turn out that light and go to sleep!' "

Mr. Marsh said, "Sounds as if it *were* time to separate you two. I thought you got along pretty well."

"Oh, we do," Amy hastened to say. "It's only once in a while— You know, Daddy"—she appealed to him— "everybody likes to be his own boss sometimes. It isn't that I don't *want* to go to sleep; but when Lin tells me to, I—"

"Get perverse, and human," Mr. Marsh twinkled. "Like the rest of us." He gave Linda's hand an affectionate squeeze. "Do you know why this job means more to me than anything else right now—aside from the personal satisfaction and having an important part in the war effort?" He didn't wait for them to answer. "It's because I can give you some of the things you should have, now
14

that you're growing up. Lin especially. A nice home in a good community—"

"What's the matter with Wayneville, New York?" Bob said belligerently. "Three cheers for good old Wayneville!"

"I thought you were getting 'sort of tired of this burg,'" Mr. Marsh reminded him mildly.

"Well, I am; but I can't hear it run down like that."

"It's all right at that, in its way," their father said. "Big, hustling, industrial . . . but a smaller town—the kind I have in mind—has a lot of pulling power right now. We all need the things it can give. I only wish your mother—" He broke off abruptly, and got up to pace back and forth.

A little silence fell on the group, their thoughts turned inward to the memory of the gentle, sweet-faced woman who had borne adversity and pain as gallantly as she had borne the happier years.

Mr. Marsh said finally, clearing his throat, "If this job turns out, there's going to be money to set aside for college for all of you who want to go—and deserve to go. And there'll be money to have help for Lin. She's been carrying too much on her shoulders."

Linda said stoutly, "I have broad shoulders." . . .

She thought, looking in the bedroom mirror now: Yes, they were broad. Much *too* broad. She was built on a big scale—not with too much weight, but with heavy bones. Wide shoulders, long arms, long legs. She had always wished she were small and daintily made. Other girls had delicate features and narrow waists and well-turned

15

wristbones. Other girls seemed to know what to do with their hands and feet, but she never did. The things she longed for, and could never have! Other girls' clothes suited them, looked gay and feminine and interesting, and hers . . . No matter what she bought, she was dissatisfied. Things looked nice in the store, or on the figure; but when she put them on, something was wrong.

"Miss Linda!" It was Mrs. Parsons again. "The grocery boy's here and he says we owe him five-seventeen."

Linda got a bill and some change out of the shabby old purse which had been her mother's, where she kept the household money. Five-seventeen. She must remember to put it down in her account book.

Mrs. Parsons took the money and turned away.

Linda called after her, "Mrs. Parsons, what about dessert for tonight?"

"Well . . ." she was reluctant. "I haven't got time to make anything fresh. We could have stewed fruit. Or maybe that cold pudding left over from last night."

"Daddy doesn't like cold pudding," Linda said firmly. "I'll come down later and make a pie."

Mrs. Parsons said nothing, but her back was eloquent. So Linda was coming down in her kitchen again to mess around! She didn't like people in her kitchen, and making a pie was just like saying her desserts weren't good enough.

Linda sighed, and returned to the contemplation of her room; but some of the pleasure had gone out of it now.

It was more of a problem, less of a joy. There were so many things to be done, and to look after! She wondered if she'd be able to do any of them properly. Living in a strange town, whose ways and shops and people she did not know, just made it harder. Her shoulders drooped in a dispirited fashion and she shrank a little from her mental glimpse of the long months ahead, full of new difficulties, each day a problem to meet.

She had come to Brookhaven with a mixture of fear and happiness. Her father, she remembered, had come home after his New York trip full of enthusiasm and high spirits. "I've found just the place for us!" he exulted. "Just the place! Ned Spears—he's a vice president—suggested I go out and look at Brookhaven; said it had everything. He gave me the name of a real estate agent, and *he* had more brains than any agent I've ever met. Listened to what I wanted and how much I could spend . . . and led me right to this house. I took it within an hour. It means a lot off my mind to know we have a place to settle in right away, and such a nice place at that."

"What's it like, Daddy, what's it like?" they chorused.

He gave them details, drew them floor plans, described everything with gestures and a voice brimming with pleasure. "It's a little shabby-looking right now, but they're painting it. And it has a garden that's gone to seed somewhat but has great possibilities. I'm itching to get on old togs and go to work in it."

"And room for a dog?" Amy said.

17

"Yes, room for a dog. Neighbors, of course, but only on one side. We've a corner lot. And there's an empty lot in back. No one's close enough to mind."

That had been the trouble in Wayneville. And there was a lake, he told the anxious Bob—a big artificial lake in one of the parks that would more than do for sailing a boat.

It was the last of July when they moved. Linda got a tired feeling just thinking of what moving had meant—gathering up their accumulated belongings, deciding what to do with things. "Oh, sell most of the old stuff," their father had said recklessly, "and we'll buy what we need down there. Just keep the best pieces, and enough for us to sleep and eat." That was exciting, but a little wearing. What to get rid of, what to keep? The house had to be left in apple-pie order for the new tenants, too, whoever they might be.

They moved away quietly. Most of their friends had gone somewhere for their vacations. Linda called up a few of her school acquaintances and bade them good-by. But there weren't many. She hadn't many friends . . . there had never been time. Amy and Bob were overjoyed at the move. New adventures, they felt, new fields! They were restless with excitement.

She owned to a feeling of excitement herself when she first glimpsed Brookhaven. Its wide, tree-shaded streets were inviting; the business district was small and conveniently located. When they saw their new home, sparkling in a fresh coat of white with gay blue shutters, they

18

had let out cries of delight. It was going to be fun—it was going to be *grand*—living in a place like this! Plans and ideas flew through Linda's mind, and her eyes flashed.

But it wasn't easy. She was still finding her way among the shops, searching out the best and most reasonable. She knew practically no one. Mrs. Parsons, engaged from an agency by her father, was put in charge and resented any interference, any instructions. Amy and Bob, with the advantage of their open natures and their youth, had found new friends almost at once and were gone all day. The house stared Linda in the face . . . so much to be done, and she hesitated to begin. She couldn't even decide on a color scheme for most of the rooms. Her father had to be gone occasionally on trips; and it was lonesome, then, with the children resenting her management, and Mrs. Parsons retiring to her room each evening in something of a sulk.

Linda would wander in the neglected garden, reading a little, sewing, darning Bob's socks, and wondering what was to happen to her in this strange town that had done nothing so far to welcome them. No one seemed to know they had moved here! Was it always going to be like this? Cliquy and standoffish? She wished with a sudden surge of homesickness for the familiarity of the narrow, cramped quarters at Wayneville; the well-known streets; the very smell of the air, heavy with smoke. At least she knew her way about there; she knew people; she knew where she stood.

Here everything was strange, and cold, and a little

forbidding by its very indifference. She'd have to go out and plunge into a new world, but she didn't want to. It would be hard to make new friends; it would be hard to be a Junior in a high school where everyone would know everyone else and probably not care about a newcomer.

"Miss Linda!" Mrs. Parsons' voice floated up the stairwell. "There's a lady here to see you."

Probably someone selling magazines, or collecting for a charity. Who else could it be? Linda flashed a glance at herself in the mirror above the chest of drawers. Her nose was shiny, and her hair needed redoing. She was a little dusty, too, from going over old boxes, but it wouldn't matter. She ran downstairs quickly. In surprise she saw that Mrs. Parsons had ushered the woman into the living room. Her visitor rose as she entered.

"I'm your neighbor," she said with a warm smile. "I'm the woman-next-door—Mrs. Clayborne."

CHAPTER TWO

SHE was a small woman, a head shorter than Linda, with a slight figure and soft, rounded features. Her smile was magnetic and Linda knew a flash of pleasure when she spoke. It was a charming voice, low and vibrant and friendly. Linda thought swiftly, "It would be lovely to have her for a friend."

But the thought was banished almost at once. Mrs. Clayborne was just being neighborly, paying her duty call, and asking if they were comfortable. After that, and when she found that Linda's mother was dead, they would not see her again, except—as they had before—briefly over the hedge.

"I've been wanting to come ever since you arrived," Mrs. Clayborne said candidly. "You've no idea how curious I've been! You all looked so busy and interesting, and such a nice family! The house has been empty much too long; and I was hoping for neighbors, and dreading them at the same time. Then, when I saw all of you, I was very happy."

Linda wanted to make a gracious little speech, too, but she felt awkward. Words stuck in her throat. It was odd,

21

in a sense, because she had seldom liked anyone better on such slight acquaintance. She watched Mrs. Clayborne in an agony of appreciation. Her movements were so easy, her gestures so graceful. Linda was conscious of her own wrists, her feet, her shiny nose. And yet Mrs. Clayborne made her feel as if *she* weren't conscious of any of these things.

"I—I think it's nice of you to call," Linda managed. That wasn't at all the way she had wanted to say it. "We've seen you, too, working in your garden. You seemed to be having such a good time!"

Mrs. Clayborne laughed. "I'm in the garden more than in the house, I'm afraid. There's always so much to be done. Or perhaps," she said whimsically, "I can always find things to do in the garden because I like to be in it."

"Oh, there is in ours, too," Linda said. Words tumbled over each other now. "We don't know where to begin. Daddy's been looking forward to working in it; but he has to be away so much, and *I* don't know what to do at all. . . . We've never had such a big garden before," she added naïvely.

"There *is* a lot to be done," Mrs. Clayborne agreed. "But that's the fun of a garden. Who would want one in which there's not a leaf to be raked or a branch to be pruned? A real gardener invents things to do, if it gets too perfect. . . . D'you know, I used to come over here, quite often, when the house was empty. I picked the roses and the chrysanthemums—because it helps them to be picked—and I covered up some of the beds with leaves,

22

and snipped around some of the bushes. But I couldn't do nearly enough; and when I heard the house was being rented, I stayed strictly on my side of the fence!"

"I wish you'd come and tell me what to do, if you love gardening!" Linda cried. "At least I could clear up a lot. . . . The trouble is, I don't know what to pull out and what to leave in."

Mrs. Clayborne laughed merrily. "I used to have a man who had a genius for pulling out plants and leaving the weeds. But I don't believe you're that way at all! Anyhow I'd love to help, or supervise—whichever you say. It will be fun to bring the garden back. It has some lovely old things in it. Have you noticed the saponaria, and the flowering quince?"

"I—" Linda began. It was hard to admit, but with Mrs. Clayborne she had to admit it. "I—well, I don't even know what a saponaria is. Or a quince, either. But I'd like to learn. . . . Oh," she said in a rush, "there are so many things to be done! We're not settled yet at all. You can see that." She waved a long arm around the room, only sparsely furnished. There were no rugs on the floor, no curtains at the windows. "It's that way all over the house. I'm going to get new things; Daddy said I might, and I want them to be right. But I don't quite know what to get, you see, or where to go."

"What fun you'll have!" Mrs. Clayborne sighed with envy. "Furnishing a house! I wish I had one to do all over again."

"Yes, but—" Linda was troubled. "I don't suppose *you*

23

would be that way, but I can't make up my mind. I never had to buy so much before, and I want it to be nice—and —and the sort of thing we can keep a long time. But I can't decide whether to have a plain rug, for instance, or a figured one; or plain hangings or flowered; or all the same kind of wood in the furniture, or different kinds. . . . That sort of thing. And I'm—well, I'm sort of afraid to choose it all by myself."

Mrs. Clayborne nodded. "Yes, I *do* know how you feel. I was that way when I married. I'd always had things done for me at home, and when I had to make my own decisions I was terrified. But I soon got over it." Her eyes twinkled. "A little authority goes a long way to building up your self-esteem. And after that, it's—well, it's a positively heady experience. I wish I had my whole house to do over again; there are so many delightful things to buy nowadays that didn't even exist when I married."

"Maybe," Linda began hesitantly, "maybe—"

"I'd help you? My dear, if you just hint at it, I'll leap at the chance. Perhaps you'd like to come over to my house first—of course I *want* you to come just as soon as you can—and you can look around and see if you approve of my taste. Then, if you do, we shall get together. Oh, what a lark it will be!"

Linda's heart was soaring. Here was a neighbor, and friendly help, and a vivid personality all in one. She began to feel, too, under the magic of Mrs. Clayborne's assurance and enthusiasm, that it would be a lark. Anyhow,

24

she would have assistance. It wouldn't *all* rest on her shoulders.

Mrs. Clayborne thought she could help in the matter of shops, too. "In fact, that was one of my reasons for coming. I thought you might like a settled resident to tell you what she had discovered by the trial-and-error method. I could save you a great deal of shopping round, I think. Living here twenty years, I've discovered which stores can be depended on and which have the best bargains. I'll give you a list this very afternoon. Or perhaps . . ." She paused in thought. "Perhaps you'd like to go downtown with me some morning, and I could point out the places and take you in to my favorites and introduce you to the managers. Would you like that?"

Linda said, gratefully, that she would. She wished she could give some little indication of her gratitude. She wished she could at least serve tea. It was sweet of Mrs. Clayborne to have come over so soon and to offer help in so many ways. Linda felt she wasn't being very hospitable, but she didn't dare go out and ask Mrs. Parsons to make tea—not in the mood Mrs. Parsons was in when last seen. There wasn't even any candy to offer her visitor.

She heard Mrs. Parsons moving ponderously down the hall from the kitchen. "I might go and see, anyhow," she thought with trepidation. Mrs. Parsons' steps continued, turned in at the living room door. Linda looked up in astonishment. She was sure her mouth fell open in utter stupefaction. It couldn't be! But it was . . . Mrs. Parsons, wearing a fresh white apron and with her hair combed back severely, was bearing a tea tray. There were cups and plates, sugar and lemon, napkins and spoons—all as it should be—and, miracle of miracles, a plate of cinnamon toast and one of small toasted cheese rolls.

Linda got hold of herself, and poured.

"My favorite favorites," Mrs. Clayborne said, smiling up at Mrs. Parsons. "And these are delicious. I remember how special they were from the time when you were with Mrs. Blanton." Mrs. Parsons beamed. "There's nothing like a cup of tea in the afternoon," Mrs. Clayborne said, sipping hers appreciatively. "It always gives me a lift. But I do admit to liking all that goes with it. A leftover from childhood days, I suppose."

"I know," Linda said, with as mature a manner as she could muster. "We always had tea when Mother—"

The little fib stuck in her throat, and mention of her mother did something to her voice. She couldn't go on.

Mrs. Clayborne said sympathetically, "You are doing a splendid job, my dear, taking charge of the household and bringing up your brother and sister. I know it must mean a great deal of work for you—and some worry too —but I do envy you. You're young, and you have young people in the house, and the rest of you are still together."

"Have you any children?" Linda asked.

"Only one. A tall, grown-up son. And he's away at camp. I lost my husband when Jerrold was a child, and it's been a lonely life in a way—except for Jerrold. I rattle around in my house these days; but I want to keep it
26

because I love it, and we were all happy there. So you can see how joyful I was to find a young family moving in next door."

Linda thought, "She has a way of making you feel that you're important." She said, in a rush, "I hope you'll always think that of us! I want you to meet Daddy, and Bob and Amy. They're nice, if I do say so myself. Bob's interested in chemistry right now. Last year it was photography, and the year before that—oh dear, what was it?"

Mrs. Clayborne said, "Mice, no doubt, or stamps, or shooting, or marble collections. It sounds like Jerrold."

"And Amy—" Linda began.

But Amy spoke for herself. There was a bang of the front screen door, a rush of footsteps, and Amy burst into the room. "Lin! Look, Lin! Can I keep him? I'm going to keep him, whatever you say. He needs somebody like me and I got him— Oh, I didn't know—" She broke off when she saw Mrs. Clayborne.

"How do you do, Amy?" their neighbor said, and Linda, horrified, cried, "Take it out—right away, Amy! It's filthy! Where in the world did you get it?"

For answer Amy hugged the bedraggled, flea-bitten, mangy puppy closer to her. Her face puckered up; her brows drew together. Linda knew that look. It was Amy's stubborn look. There was no use arguing with her . . . now. She seemed like a docile child; but once she had set her mind on a thing, there was no budging her. And stray animals and lost pets were her passion.

27

"I kept telling you I wanted a dog—"

"Yes, dear, and Daddy said you could get one as soon as we found a kennel—"

"We've been here nearly two weeks and you haven't found one yet. I told Grace and Bill about it, and they said why didn't we go to the pound? So we did. . . . It's *full* of dogs! I had a terrible time making up my mind. But this one"—she looked down and her face smoothed out and a smile curved her mouth—"this one, Lin, needed me most. It makes me *sick* to think people let their dogs get like this. The man said he was nearly dead when he picked him up, and he was glad to get rid of him 'cause he's got so many fleas and—and things. So he said I could have him for fifty cents. And I took him right away before he changed his mind. But, of course, he said not to forget I've got to get a license. The license'll be two-fifty."

"And where did you get the fifty cents?" Linda asked.

"I borrowed it off Grace. Grace borrowed it off her mother. I said I'd bring it right over. Lin, I've got to have this dog! He's just right for me!"

"What—what kind is it?"

"Mostly wire-haired terrier, I think. It's sort of mixed, the man said. Isn't he cute? I mean he will be when I get him washed and combed and fixed up."

"I know a wonderful flea powder," Mrs. Clayborne put in. "We used to use it on our dog when he went off and mingled with others and brought home the results."

"Oh, would you tell me? Lin could get some. . . . Or

28

I'll go down and get it right away. That is— How much is it?"

Amy remembered that the money question was important now. She couldn't get in too deep.

"Perhaps I have some left. It will still be good. Anyhow, you might try it if Linda lets you keep him."

Amy rushed over to her sister. "Lin, please! I'll keep him outside till he's cured, and I'll take care of him all by myself. And I'll feed him and everything. He won't eat much. Not at first. And he can have my table scraps."

"If any!" Linda had to laugh.

"Well, I'll save some of my dinner for him. And I'll pay for him, too, myself, if you'll just let me have the money now."

"How will you pay for him?" Linda wanted to know.

Amy was ready for her. "I'll make all the beds every day for a week, and run extra errands, and—and help in the garden. Maybe Mrs. Clayborne has some work I could do, too, if that's not enough," she said hopefully.

"Amy!" Linda was aghast.

But Mrs. Clayborne said at once, "I'm sure I can find something. Let me know how you're making out. And come over for the flea powder whenever you like."

"I think he's a bargain," Amy said proudly. "I'll bet you won't know him in a couple of weeks." Just then the poor puppy gave itself a long, miserable scratching. "Well —or months," Amy amended. "I'm going to be a vet— a vet'narian," she brought out triumphantly.

29

"A veterinarian," Linda corrected.

"Yes. Anyhow," she said, appealing to Mrs. Clayborne, "you know—an animal doctor."

"Take him out now," Linda said sternly. "He's one mass of bites."

"But what about the *money?* I've got to pay Grace."

"You can take fifty cents out of my household purse," Linda said. "And tie him outside." Amy nodded and skipped out, hugging the puppy close. Linda sighed. What a way to introduce Amy! "I'm sorry—" she began.

"She's an enchanting child. So serious. Is she always so serious?"

Linda said, with a rueful smile, "She's determined. Amy knows what she wants, and she almost always gets it. Sometimes I wonder what I—"

The screen door crashed to with an especially loud bang. In the hallway stood Bob, his hair plastered over his forehead, a red welt on one cheek, and water dripping from his torn shirt and trousers.

"I was sailing my boat. And, boy, does she sail! She's the best on the lake."

"Bob, you're dripping!"

"Oh, I fell in," he offered carelessly. "It wasn't anything. Guess I leaned over too far."

"Well, go and wipe your shoes and wring your trousers. Mrs. Parsons won't like mud all over the floors. And take a bath and change," Linda said shortly, a flush of embarrassment on her cheeks.

"Sure," he agreed. "What did you think—I was going to stay like this? Gee! What are those things?"

"Go on now, Bob."

"Smells like cheese. Gosh, they look good. Gimme a couple, Lin, and I'll beat it."

Linda said crossly, "When you're changed you can have some. Not before."

"Okay." He went off whistling.

"*Out*side first," Linda called after him. The screen door banged. Linda looked helplessly at Mrs. Clayborne. "I didn't want to introduce him when he was in such a state," she apologized.

"My dear, boys are seldom in a state to be introduced!" Mrs. Clayborne laughed. "Jerrold always seemed to have rolled in the mud or be carrying snakes or showing the marks of a fight whenever I had guests." She rose. "And now I can scarcely recognize him—he's the acme of neatness in his uniform! I must be going. It's been such a nice visit, and such a lovely tea."

Linda walked with her to the door. "I'm glad you came," she said impulsively.

"So am I," Mrs. Clayborne returned. "Remember to call me if you need any help . . . but do come before that!"

Turning back into the house, Linda wished vainly that things might have gone as smoothly as such a pleasant caller deserved. The tea had started off the afternoon well enough, but Amy and Bob had certainly spoiled any effect she might have built up. Of course, Mrs. Clayborne hadn't

31

seemed to mind; but she was a woman of the world, trained to disregard that sort of thing.

Linda picked up the tea tray and took it into the kitchen. Mrs. Parsons was grinding meat in the chopper. "Thank you for fixing tea," Linda said to her uncompromising back. "I was just wishing for it when you came in. It was such a nice surprise!"

She took two cheese rolls and a piece of cinnamon toast and laid them aside for Bob. He shouldn't have them, after the way he'd acted, but she had promised.

Mrs. Parsons turned around, her arms on her hips. "I always fix tea for ladies like that," she said. "I know what's expected of me."

But her voice belied her rather harsh words. She was pleased at Linda's praise.

"I—I know how busy you've been all afternoon. That's why I didn't ask for it," Linda said. She gave a swift glance at the kitchen clock hanging above the sink. "I'd have time to fix a pie for supper if I start right away."

"There's no need," Mrs. Parsons said. "If you don't want the cold pudding, I could make up a batch of blueberry muffins . . . they don't take long."

Linda controlled her surprise. "That would be lovely! We're all crazy about blueberry muffins."

"So I've noticed," Mrs. Parsons said, with a kind of grim pleasure. "There's never any left . . . which is as it should be," she added.

Linda thought dazedly, "Why, she's a different woman! Just because I praised her a little!" She remembered the way Mrs. Parsons had beamed when Mrs. Clayborne mentioned her cheese rolls. That was all she needed—a pat on the back, a pleasant word. "I'll try to keep that in mind," Linda decided humbly.

She was more determined now than ever to speak to Bob in Mrs. Parsons' behalf. "You'll have to stop experimenting in your room at night," she told him when he came down again, slicked and fairly clean. "Mrs. Parsons can't sleep on account of the smells. And, besides, you are supposed to go to bed when you go up."

He stuck his hands in his pockets; his face went sullen. "I'm going to be a chemist," he said belligerently. "How do you think a fellow is going to get anywhere in chemistry if he doesn't experiment?"

"You can do it in the daytime," she said firmly.

"I've got other things to do then. And, besides, it's my room—I can do what I like in it."

"Oh no, you can't, Bob. It may be your room; but it's our house, and everybody in it has to be considered."

"Well, old Parsons doesn't. She can take a nap in the afternoon, or sleep with a gas mask." He laughed suddenly at the picture this brought up.

"Stop talking nonsense!" Linda said with vehemence. "You're just stalling. I said you'll have to stop experimenting up there at night, and I mean it."

"Old Whiny-Voice!" he taunted. " 'I said you'll have to stop, and I mean it!' "

His voice was a startling imitation of her own. Whenever he wanted to tease her, or when he was being repri-

33

manded, he made use of this ability of his to mock her. Old Whiny-Voice. They often told her that her voice had a whine to it, a queer hardness; but she couldn't help it. It was mean of Bob to taunt her just because she was losing her temper. She flushed up with anger.

"Never mind my voice. I'm telling you what to do. You can clear all those bottles and tubes out of your room and that will put an end to the whole business."

That shocked him. "Aw, Lin, have a heart! I'm not doing anybody any harm——"

"Just robbing Mrs. Parsons of her sleep, that's all," Linda retorted. "She said she wouldn't put up with it any longer."

"Oh, *she* said, did she? Well, I'll speak to Dad tonight. I'm not going to be bossed by any Mrs. Parsons—or by you, either. Gosh, it's getting so a fellow can't do anything around here!"

Linda wanted to call after him, but held back. She frowned in distaste. It was horrid to have Amy and Bob running to their father in defiance, or in a bid for sympathy. She hated being the stern disciplinarian, the one who had to forbid and to enforce. It made her seem less a sister than a martinet . . . and she didn't want Amy and Bob to grow away from her. Sometimes she was at a loss which way to turn, or what to do. Like this. She knew how Bob felt about his experiments; how important they were to him, at least momentarily. She liked having him interested in something so worth while; for herself, she would have let him go. But they couldn't afford to antagonize

34

Mrs. Parsons . . . and, after all, her complaint was reasonable enough. Linda had wanted to put it calmly and sensibly before Bob, so that he would see it as she did. But his sullen resentment at her first words had made her cross; and then his harsh imitation of her, calling her Old Whiny-Voice, had settled the matter. Anger never got her anywhere, she knew that. But she couldn't help it.

Bob lost no time in voicing his grievance at dinner. He hardly waited for Mrs. Parsons to put the food on the table before he was off. Words spilled over each other in his hurt resentment; he flung a swift look of triumph at Linda.

"She says I've got to quit experimenting. And I don't have to, do I, Dad?"

Mr. Marsh looked from one to the other. "What is all this?"

Linda and Bob began talking at once; their voices rose higher and higher, each trying to drown out the other.

"Wait a minute! One at a time," Mr. Marsh begged. "Let's get the facts. You first, Linda."

He listened gravely while they told him. Then he deliberated a moment. "It doesn't strike me as so much of a problem," he said. "I think Mrs. Parsons has something there . . . seems to me I've been haunted by a sulphuric ghost a couple of nights myself. . . . And Linda's right to ask you to clear out—"

"Aw, Dad! Aw, gee, I never thought—"

"But that doesn't mean," he continued calmly, "that you have to give up being a chemist."

35

"Well, where am I going to do it, for Pete's sake? Where am I going to have room—"

"What about the cellar?" their father asked mildly. They both stared at him, agape. "Lots of room down there. We could partition off a place under one of the windows, put up some shelves—" Bob's face glowed. "Or, still better, how about knocking up a little shed in the garden? Say, back of the high syringa bush. It wouldn't be an eyesore there, and our chemist would have a real laboratory. There's some lumber in the cellar we could use. Maybe Bob would put up the shack all by himself . . . with a little engineering advice. How about it?"

Bob leaped up, his grin from ear to ear. "Gosh, Dad, that's swell! That's just what I want! A place to myself where I can get away—" He broke off, a little sheepishly. "You know how it is. You just get in the midst of something and you hate to be called off . . ."

"Sure," Mr. Marsh said. "The greatest inventions require concentration and a certain amount of—ah, privacy. And, at the same time, the smells can evaporate in the outside air, and Mrs. Parsons can get her sleep, and Linda won't have to worry any more."

How simple it had been! Why hadn't *she* thought of a solution like that, and earned Bob's gratitude instead of his resentment? Maybe as you grew older it was easier. Their father had hit on the one right answer without any difficulty. He saw all sides of the question; and when you saw all sides, he had once told her, an answer was always forthcoming.

36

Amy had been listening to the conversation with ill-concealed impatience. "When you people get through talking—" she began.

Mr. Marsh smiled at her. "What's on *your* mind, Amy?"

She leaped up and down in her excitement. "I want you to come and see my dog!" she cried. "He's all washed and deflead—"

"Where did you get the powder?" Linda could not keep from asking.

"Oh, I stopped right in at Mrs. Clayborne's on my way home and got it. Almost a whole canful! And it certainly worked. . . . Daddy, be sure and save some of that lumber. I've got him in a carton now; but I want you to build him a doghouse, so I can keep him in the yard. He's going to be an outdoor dog," she announced firmly. "I read that it's best, and that way he won't bother Mrs. Parsons—much."

Their father said, with a twinkle, "Bring him on. You certainly work fast, Amy."

And Bob, still grinning, offered magnanimously, "Listen, kid, when I get through building my shack *I'll* make you a doghouse."

CHAPTER THREE

THE days were busy after that. Bob hammered and sawed happily behind the syringa, Amy was importantly exercising a painfully clean wire-haired that she had named Jinks, and Linda spent morning after morning with Mrs. Clayborne learning the shops.

The neighborly friendship had developed rapidly. Linda and Mary Clayborne worked in the garden together, and it was assuming a neat and orderly appearance under their joint onslaught. Grubby and happy, they would have lunch together under the apple tree and then pore over catalogues and magazines.

Mary Clayborne's own house, Linda discovered, was delightful. Linda had thought it a little quiet at first, and reserved, but she soon discovered that it grew on her. She liked to go there, because it was restful and friendly and there were always little surprises to hold your interest. It was like Mrs. Clayborne herself, she decided.

The rooms were full of light and air and a sense of space. Fine old mahogany glowed with a satin sheen. Rugs were so well chosen that Linda couldn't quite remember, when she went home that first time, what they were—she only knew that they were right. There were books in open shelves, and odd bits from different parts of the world—vases and figurines and brasses—on mantelpiece and side tables. A piece of old brocade over the piano. A delicate water color in a good light. A flower arrangement above the fireplace. A carved sconce, an old mirror . . . something to delight the eye wherever you looked. And, in every room, some photograph of Jerrold, from a laughing boy to a handsome young man with aviator's wings on his tunic.

"You must forgive me these," Mary Clayborne said. "They're a mother's way of keeping her son with her."

"But we can't have a house like this," Linda protested. She wanted to say that it would cost too much, and take too long.

"Of course not," Mrs. Clayborne agreed. "You don't want a house like mine. This place is Me. You want a house that's You—all of you. The thing to do," she added, "is to make a picture of what you want your house to be; and then we'll go at it, piece by piece. The general effect first. What do you want your house to represent?"

"Well," Linda said slowly, for this was a new idea to her, "I want it light and airy—like yours. Then it ought to be a place where Amy and Bob can feel free to entertain their friends, if they want to, and do the things they like."

She felt safe there; Bob had his chemistry shack, and she doubted if any new hobby would be quite as messy and smelly.

39

Mrs. Clayborne nodded. "Go on."

"And we ought to have furniture that's easy to keep clean, and that won't show too many marks. And I want cheerful curtains, and plenty of lamps so we don't have to crowd in one spot to read. And—"

"That's enough to start on."

"But the color schemes! I just don't know what to have —where!" Linda sounded despairing.

It wasn't so difficult, after all. Not under Mrs. Clayborne's expert guidance and deft suggestions. The magazines helped; they found rooms that pleased them, and then analyzed why they were pleased. They chose a piece of furniture and built a corner around it; shopped for curtains and found the one right pattern; decided on small rugs that could be rearranged or rolled up as the occasion demanded; bought tables for lamps, and then the lamps themselves. Gradually the rooms took on a lived-in, inviting air.

Linda, by this time, had definite ideas about her own room. Mrs. Clayborne had said she ought to choose a color that made her happy and then build around that, and she had decided on a peachy-apricot shade that pleased her every time she opened her eyes or entered the room. The walls seemed to hold sunlight, and the sheer window curtains brought in the air. She had her blue bedspread and a tufted slipper chair and her maple writing desk. Amy had been allowed to do her own room, too. Linda shook her head over it, but Amy was satisfied. There was a severe desk with a green-shaded student

40

lamp, and a row of books—*The Care and Training of Dogs, Diseases of Canines, How to Judge Dogs*—propped against the wall. A highboy supported her toilet set and a row of bottles containing dog medicines.

"Don't you want a mirror?" Linda asked, but Amy said, "There's a mirror in the bathroom."

Mrs. Clayborne took Linda to New York several times; and they prowled in secondhand stores and auction rooms, coming back with "loot" that was surprisingly reasonable and just what they wanted. Mr. Marsh was delighted with the effect Linda was achieving. He liked the smooth, blond wood table, the adjustable bookshelves and ottoman she had chosen, and puffed his pipe contentedly as he gazed around the cheerful, well-lighted room.

"I won't want to leave this place," he said. "And I'll have to. Another trip in the offing—a long one this time."

"Anyhow, you'll want to come back." Linda laughed. "It sounds just like an advertisement—the home you don't want to leave."

"Of course the occupants might have something to do with my wanting to come back," he said whimsically. He looked at his daughter. "Happy, Lin?"

The smile died from her face, and she turned her back so that he could not watch her expression. Happy wasn't the word; she'd been too busy, really, to think just how she felt. But she knew she wasn't happy. She was waiting . . . waiting for her new life to begin. This was just a prelude. It was pleasant to have this house to do over, to

41

have Mrs. Clayborne's friendly assistance. But it wasn't all of life. What was there to be for *her* in this new environment, this whole new existence? She wanted friends of her own, activities into which she could throw herself wholeheartedly; she wanted to be part of a circle, tight-knit and demanding. She wanted a bevy of her contemporaries to laugh with and work with. That was still to come. She hoped it was still to come. There hadn't been time enough in Wayneville; now there would be *time*. But would they want her, would they welcome her?

She had waited too long to answer.

Her father said anxiously, "What's the matter, Lin?"

"Of course I'm happy," she managed. Her voice had the whiny note that it always had, intensified now by her effort to sound spontaneous. It wasn't convincing. She repeated, "Of course I'm happy here," as if by repetition she could make it so.

Only it was like whistling in the dark. She wasn't at all sure . . . and something that happened the next day made her still more unsure.

Mrs. Clayborne had invited the Marshes to an outdoor supper party. Linda helped arrange the table under the arbor, and spread it with a striped linen cloth and yellow napkins. There was a salad made up in the pantry, and rolls slit and buttered, and hamburgers molded into cakes waiting to be grilled at the open fireplace. Everything seemed complete, but Mrs. Clayborne had an idea.

"Let's walk down to the Dainty Shoppe and get some ice cream. We can keep it in the refrigerator tray till we're ready. I feel just like some strawberry! How about you?"

"Chocolate every time," Linda said. "But whatever you say."

They started off gaily, in the late summer afternoon. Sprinklers twirled on emerald lawns; a few cars whizzed by; an airplane circled distantly overhead. Linda liked this street, liked Brookhaven. The houses were set far apart and all had a comfortable air. Two boys were approaching—tall, well-built boys, one with flaming red hair.

Mrs. Clayborne exclaimed, "Why, there's Ben and Jimmy! I've been wanting them to meet you. How nice!" The boys hailed her, with respectful familiarity, and she performed introductions. "Ben Brixton, you might as well know, is known as Carrots . . . for obvious reasons. He's practically a neighbor of yours—lives in that white house halfway down the block. And Jimmy Post is something of a neighbor in the opposite direction."

Linda was glad she had just done her hair in the smooth hard roll she had practiced so long; every hair was in place, built up over her high rounded forehead and pulled back from above her ears. And she was wearing a new dress which had appealed to her. It was striped and sheer, with a full gathered skirt and ruffled at neck and sleeves.

The boys obediently acknowledged her presence. One fleeting, comprehensive look, and their gaze went back to Mrs. Clayborne.

"Linda will be in your class at school. She'll be a Junior. You'll be seeing a lot of each other."

That was a pleasant prospect. Linda's eyes lighted.

"Yes," Jimmy Post said unenthusiastically, after a little pause. "Uh—what do you hear from Jerrold, Mrs. Clayborne? Has he shot down any Japs yet?"

"Oh, Jerrold's still teaching at camp. He fumes about it, of course, but they say they need him where he is."

"He's a swell teacher, too," Ben put in. "Luke—you know, Luke Peabody—said he knows his stuff. Luke got his wings last week, and Jerrold taught him last year at the field."

Mary Clayborne's eyes lighted at this praise of her son. "Listen, boys, I've an idea. Can't you both come to supper tonight? I'm having a hamburger grill in the garden— very informal."

"That would be great!" they said, almost together.

"Linda's coming, too—her whole family. In fact, it's *for* Linda and her family."

Linda, waiting with a hopeful heart, saw the change that came over their faces. Ben scuffed his foot against the curbstone; Jimmy tossed his racket in the air and caught it.

"That would be swell, Mrs. Clayborne. Thanks," Ben said finally. "But—well, I don't know about Jim; but I've got a date. Family stuff."

Jimmy said, a little too hurriedly, "Same here. That is, Mother wants me to do some errands before I meet Dad; and she spoke of our going to the Club for dinner."

Mrs. Clayborne said easily, "Well, some other time,

44

perhaps? I hardly thought I'd have the luck to get you both on such short notice."

Ben said, "Some other time? You bet. And thanks, Mrs. Clayborne. Well, Jim, we'd better be moving. 'By," they said to Mrs. Clayborne, and then, after a moment, they flung over their shoulders, "Good-by," to Linda.

The hot color flew up into Linda's face. She could feel it spreading to her hairline; her pulse throbbed in her temples. She had seldom been so near to crying—crying with rage and disappointment. They had been going to accept . . . until they knew she was to be there. They had scarcely noticed her in the first place, but they had seen enough of her to know that they didn't want to come if she was to be there. Her lips trembled and she winked rapidly, seeing the pleasant Brookhaven street through a red haze.

Mrs. Clayborne was saying, "Too bad! But you'll get to know them soon enough at school. Only I had thought it would be nice— Ben's a fine chap; he was president of his class last year, and he's an all-round kind of boy. And Jimmy Post is a track star, aside from being quite an organizer, they tell me."

Linda mumbled something; she didn't know what. They hadn't liked her; she didn't even rate a second glance from them. And these were prominent boys at school, leaders in their field. If they didn't like her, it followed that others wouldn't either . . . not the ones she wanted to have like her.

She felt a dull ache, a kind of despair. School hadn't even begun, and yet she had a foretaste of what the year would be. Ignored, unhappy, outside the circle. It wasn't that she had expected to be popular all at once, to walk into school life and have it immediately revolve around her. But if two of the leading boys met her and hardly knew she existed . . . so that they had to remember with an effort to say "Good-by" to her when they left her presence— Oh, it was horrible!

"I can't face a school like that," she thought desperately. "What's wrong with me? I'm not perfect, I know. But what's wrong? If I only *knew!*" Just now, for instance . . . Hadn't she been cordial enough? She hadn't said much, but then she hadn't had an opportunity to. And she had looked interested and eager, she was sure of that. Perhaps too interested, too eager.

Anyhow, she hadn't rated with them. Why not, was a puzzle. It hurt to admit it and, admitting it, she could feel her spirits sinking to her slippers. Oh, if September never came! It might be a little lonely this way, but at school it would be torture. To be surrounded by people who didn't know you existed or, knowing it, who ignored you!

The pleasant outdoor supper passed like a slow dream; a kind of nightmare to live through, trying to seem gay and lighthearted and grateful when her thoughts were all gloomy and dispiriting. The salad stuck in her throat . . . she caught her father looking at her quizzically several times, and once he asked in a low voice, "Why so droopy, Lin? The heat getting you?"

Amy and Bob were in their element, grilling the hamburgers, passing the rolls, digging in with healthy young appetites and showing their appreciation with noisy groans of delight. Jinks sat up and begged for bits of meat, and Amy proudly put him through his paces.

"See, I knew he was a bargain dog! I think maybe he had circus performers or something for his grandmother and grandfather. You only have to tell him two or three times and he gets a new trick. Of course, I don't want him to be just a *trick* dog," she said righteously, but her proud manner was that of a parent with a particularly brilliant child.

Linda thought that the evening she had looked forward to with such pleasure would never end. Her father was in no hurry to go home, and Amy and Bob were enchanted with the opportunity to stay up later than usual. But Linda longed to be alone in her room, face to face with this new problem which she did not know how to handle.

If there were only someone she could talk it over with! But it was hard to know how to begin. Her father, she knew, would gently pooh-pooh the idea that his daughter wasn't as good, as popular, as welcome, as the next one. Mrs. Clayborne might have helped; but the day after the party she came over to announce, with flushed face and bright eyes, that she had received a telegram from Jerrold.

"He's wangled a little leave—very unexpectedly, and there isn't time to come all the way back here; so he wants me to meet him in Savannah. We have friends there, and it's only a short distance from the camp. I'm going down on the midnight, and I'm as excited about it as a girl!"

"How long will you be gone?" Linda asked, struggling between happiness for her neighbor's joy and a new sense of loneliness.

"Oh, just as long as he can manage it . . . probably till after Labor Day, anyway," Mary Clayborne said. "And then I may stay on a week or so visiting with my friends. They're long-suffering and will put me up for whatever time I can stay."

So Mrs. Clayborne would be gone until after school opened. Linda hadn't realized, until that moment, how much she had been counting on the possibility of a little get-together at her neighbor's with the new boys. Perhaps if they had known her better, if she could have met them on more familiar ground, if there had just been a chance— But that was gone now; and in school they'd have no time for her, remembering their first impression.

Elementary school began two days before high school. Linda took Amy and Bob, in her father's absence, interviewed their teachers, and saw them happily settled in their classes. Bob made friends easily, and Amy had four little friends in her group. They scarcely noticed when she left them. They didn't need her, and she could see how excited they were at the prospect of the new school year.

She went with leaden feet, and a pounding heart, to register herself at high school that opening day. It was a pleasant building in Georgian style, with windows glittering in the sun and a flag billowing proudly from a high pole in front of the circular walk. Converging lines of girls and boys, laughing and talking together, streamed up the walk and through the gracious doors. Linda felt more alone than ever. She found the principal's office and sat in the outer room while one case after another was disposed of. Eventually her turn came and she was ushered into Mr. Galbraith's presence by a crisply efficient secretary.

She presented her report cards and letter from her former school, and Mr. Galbraith scanned them carefully. "They seem quite satisfactory. What are you planning to take here? Junior year, as you know, permits you to make a choice and to begin your majoring."

"I'd been taking a general course," Linda said ineffectively. "I hadn't thought—"

"Are you planning to go to college?"

College! It was the bright dream in most girls' lives! There would be money for it now, she knew; the halls of learning beckoned from east and west, north and south. For most people it was merely a matter of choosing where they would be happiest and where they could pursue what they had decided upon. But she turned her head away. If high school continued to be as unsatisfactory and unpleasant an experience as it had been in Wayneville, and as she felt sure it would be here, she could not see herself taking on four more years of that sort of thing. She would try to live through these coming terms, and then there would be an end of it.

"College?" she repeated. "I might have . . . but I've decided now not to go."

The principal raised his eyebrows, not in surprise but in interrogation. "That's a bit unusual. I suppose, however, that you have your heart set on a career of some kind—or on entering war work, as so many of our girls are doing now?"

"No," said Linda painfully. "That is, it may turn into something of that kind; but I hadn't planned on it. You see, I don't have any particular bent or talent . . . and I'm needed at home."

"Well, that will work out of itself. If you want to enter college, though, it's well to keep that goal in mind so we can plan your studies accordingly."

"I don't want to go to college," Linda said loudly.

It struck her, with a horrified sense of astonishment, that her voice was unnecessarily loud, as if she were defying someone. And he was just trying to be helpful.

"We have scholarships, you know, to take care of deserving pupils, and that offer a nice little financial help," he went on. He glanced again at her cards from Wayneville. "I think you're college material. It would be rather a pity not to get ready for the eventuality, even though, later on, you decided not to go. In that way you'd be prepared, and if the opportunity came you could grasp it. Sometimes," he said deliberately, looking at her in a kindly fashion, "we change our minds when it's too late— or at least inconvenient."

Linda saw his point; and she had no argument against it, except that she was sure she wouldn't want to go to college when the time came. Still, she supposed she might as well take college preparatory subjects, because she had no special desire in any field and college preparatory subjects would probably make as interesting a curriculum as any. She listened attentively while he outlined the course and worked up her studies. English; Latin (she might as well continue the Latin she had had in Wayneville); Spanish, because that was the coming modern language and a knowledge of it would not be amiss in any case; history, of course. American? European? She decided on European, and took the additional one-period Current Events. Things were happening so rapidly, so breath-takingly, in the world of today that she felt she couldn't ever be adequately informed. And anyway, she told the principal with a shy smile, it was exciting to live with history in the making.

He nodded approvingly. "I'm glad you feel that way. Too many people see only the inconvenience, or the horror, or the sadness. But all life becomes history, and to have a part in the most stupendous history-making of all time is a privilege, I think. A chance to understand, and

51

to work for a better world, and to serve the world we're living in."

To round out her program she took chemistry—Bob would smile at that, she thought briefly—and two periods of art.

Mr. Galbraith stood up and shook her by the hand. "I hope you'll be happy here," he said. "We have one of the finest schools in the state. But not everything revolves around teachers and equipment and buildings. It's the people who make use of these things, and contribute to them as well. Come to me if you run into any snags."

Linda spent the rest of the short day meeting her teachers—Miss Lovett, Mr. Hopewell, Mr. Newton, Miss Kittredge—trying to disentangle a blur of new faces and catalogue them, hunting her way from class to class, getting lost and being directed by the students with armbands and important airs who manned the corridors. The halls were full of girls arm in arm, boys careening by and guffawing, calling to one another. Everybody seemed to know everybody else. Linda had expected this was the way it would be—new and lonely and confusing —but underneath she had hoped differently. Somewhere there should have been a friendly, inquiring girl her own age—someone whose interest was aroused at sight of her. Somewhere there should have been a place for her.

The first day, of course, was always discouraging. Freshmen looking like frightened rabbits, darting here and there and squeaking, "Please, is 7-B on *this* floor? I've been around and around—" Older classmen swaggering with importance, making dates. The bulletin board, before which Linda stood as long as she dared, had an attractive list of events already posted: invitations to join clubs, track and community affairs, a concert to be held in the auditorium . . .

Fragments of conversation reached her from those who drifted up to read carelessly and comment: "Oh gosh, chess again! Why not a jitterbug contest—something that would *get* you somewhere?" "Listen, if you think George Holden isn't the best all-round athlete this school's ever had—" "I bet the Seniors will have to usher again at Miss Dingle's musical evenings! Me, I'm going to be sick every time one rolls around!" "Let's go down to the Dainty Shoppe—I could eat a couple of nuts with a dash of ice cream on top."

She wished she were a part of some group, however small. She saw a dozen girls who looked attractive and full of spirit, but they did not see her. By keeping her eyes peeled for Ben or Jimmy, she managed to spy Ben directing traffic on one of the stairs. But he did not see her . . . at least when his eyes met hers briefly, he looked through and beyond her.

Her father said at dinner that night, "How'd everybody make out today?"

That was the cue for Bob and Amy to launch into graphic, spirited accounts of their new life, and Linda listened enviously. How easy it was for them!

"What about you, Lin?" her father persisted, when he had stemmed the vociferous tide of their enthusiasm.

53

She looked down at her plate. "Oh—well, at first it's a little confusing, you know. I spent most of the day getting straightened out and going to various classes, and there's a conflict in my schedule—"

"Well, that'll all work out," he said, in comfortable ignorance. "I was talking to Mr. Price on the train. He said the school system here is among the finest."

The school system! You couldn't be happy with a school system, even though it was the finest in the world! You were happy only when you fitted into a circle; when you had friends your own age; when you felt you were wanted, and were a part of what was going on.

The sense of strangeness wore off, in the following week, as Linda learned her way around and the scenes grew familiar to her; but the sense of loneliness persisted, stronger than before, because now it was confirmed by each new day.

In Wayneville she had hurried home because she was needed; here she hurried home—because she was not wanted. She realized that her particular case was somewhat different. It was because she was entering the Junior class as a stranger, when nearly everyone in it was acquainted through at least two years' daily intercourse. If she could have been a Freshman . . . Freshmen got acquainted with one another as they got acquainted with the school. They were new and strange to conditions, even though they had lived in the town. She had the double disadvantage of being from out of town and entering

54

a class where friendships and groups had already been formed.

Oh, she saw how it was! But she brooded about it just the same. On a warm, sunny afternoon when everyone was out at the field watching a tennis match she stood in front of her mirror, staring with rebellious eyes at her reflection. "I'll bet I haven't said more than two words to three people this whole week," she thought miserably. "Outside of teachers." The afternoon stretched ahead of her in unending boredom. Mrs. Parsons was rolling out a pie, and was not to be disturbed; Amy and Bob were in the park. The house was unnaturally quiet. Mrs. Clayborne had just come home; it would be better to wait a day or so, hungry as she was for her companionship, before she went over, until Mrs. Clayborne had had time to unpack and get settled again.

What was there to do—except wash her hair and take a sun bath? She put on her scarlet bathing suit and tied up her wet head in a Turkish towel. "I'll read while I sun my hair," she decided. She didn't want to read—she wanted to talk to someone her own age.

The garden was really looking lovely, after its short but concentrated care, and Linda was proud of it. She was proud of their new home, too—she wanted to share it. She chose a sunny spot and spread out an old blanket. The sun was warm and relaxing and she lay staring up into the treetops, combing her hair with idle fingers.

"Lazybones! You look too comfortable for words!"

It was Mary Clayborne's laughing voice coming over the hedge.

Linda jumped up with a cry of pleasure. "I'm so *glad* you're back; I've missed you!"

"Have you?" Mrs. Clayborne said warmly. "I didn't dare hope I could compete with all your new friends at school. Have you made a great many?"

"It's—still early yet. I'm just finding my way around," Linda said guardedly. She could not confess her failure.

"Of course!" Mrs. Clayborne seemed to think the explanation entirely plausible. "My dear, I must tell you how lovely you look with your hair hanging that way! I had no idea you were lucky enough to have such a soft wave. Is it natural?"

Linda nodded. "I've always had it. Not a curl, really, just a—a ripple."

"But who would have thought it, the way you wear it— so stiff and rolled! And most girls would give their eye-teeth to have what you have. Come here this minute," she ordered. "I have an idea."

"I look a mess," Linda said humbly. "My hair's flying all over, and this suit—I thought it was such a lovely color when I bought it, but it makes me look like a green pea."

"It's a hard color to wear, except for very light-skinned people," Mrs. Clayborne suggested. "You can wear red, but it has to be a darker, richer tone. With hair like yours, Linda, you have to play up to it, not kill it with color."

Linda slipped on a robe and came through the hedge.

56

"Sit down. I adore playing with hair. I should have been a hairdresser." Mrs. Clayborne took the brush from Linda's hand and brushed vigorously, with long, smooth strokes, till the hair glistened in the sun and stood out in a fluffy, light mass. The ends curled just below Linda's shoulder. Mrs. Clayborne parted the hair halfway back and turned under the front mass so that it formed a soft bang. She stood off, holding it in place with one hand, and viewed her handiwork. "It's perfect! Come and see if you don't like it."

Cautiously they made their way into the house and found a mirror.

Linda stared at herself in astonishment. "Why—why, I look like another person!"

"Oh, I wouldn't want you to look like someone else," Mrs. Clayborne protested. "But this—don't you think this suits you better? And see how it brings out your lovely eyes."

No one had told Linda that she had lovely eyes—though she had always thought of them as her "least worst" feature—and she felt a glow of pride. Mrs. Clayborne's new hair arrangement was a sort of miracle; it transformed her face, giving it a golden-brown frame and making it seem narrower and more pointed; and the curve of hair over her forehead cut the height and focused attention on her eyes.

"Here's a scissors," Linda said suddenly. "Cut it off just as you have it."

With a little urging, Mrs. Clayborne did so. The fringe

57

was fluffy and full; and Linda, pirouetting before the glass to see all angles, had a lift of pride in her appearance. It was exciting to evolve a new appearance with just your regular equipment! She looked different—maybe she would feel different and act different, too. All kinds of things might happen!

Linda said in excitement, whirling around, "Tell me about your trip; I haven't heard a word. I've been a pig —but *you* made me that way."

Mrs. Clayborne laughed. "Oh, you'll be hearing about the trip and Jerrold for weeks. Just now it's much more thrilling to sit back and contemplate my creation."

Looking at her watch, Linda gave a start. "Good heavens, the afternoon's flown! I'll be late meeting Daddy." She leaned across the dressing table and planted a swift kiss on Mrs. Clayborne's cheek. "Thanks a million!"

She dressed in a rush, cast a comprehensive glance over the table to see if everything was in place, and then was out of the house and down the street. It was more than half a mile to the station and, covering the last two blocks, she heard the train pulling in. Her father liked to find one or the other standing on the platform scanning the windows and waving at first sight of him, and she spurted down the street and up the ramp leading to the little suburban station in its setting of green.

A boy on a bicycle swooped around the corner and she did an agile side step.

"Sorry!" he sang out. Then, with an amazed second

look, he put out his foot and braked the bike to an abrupt halt. "Why, it's Linda! Hiya, Linda. I swear I didn't know you there for a minute."

"Hi, Ben," Linda said breathlessly.

"You—uh, why, you look swell tonight, Linda!" There was real conviction in his voice, and Linda heard it.

She said happily, "Thanks. I can't stop. Dad's train is in."

She ran on, conscious that he was still staring after her as she raced up the hill.

"Well, Lin, you look as if you'd been doing a daily dozen!" her father greeted her as he swung off the platform and gave her a hearty kiss and his folded paper. "Color in the cheeks, sparkle in the eyes—" She waited, holding her breath, for him to notice the new hair-do and comment on it. But his eyes dwelt only on her flushed, excited face. "And a sort of—well, happy look that I *like* to see. What's the news?"

She took his arm and they walked slowly homeward together. He had noticed her new radiance, her pleasure in her appearance; but he hadn't noticed what had caused it. It gave her a secret amusement, and she hugged it to her.

Amy and Bob, however, fell upon the transformation with howls and whistles of amazement.

"For Pete's sake," Bob said, "whyn't you do it before?" And Amy, arms akimbo, her serious little face concentrated and grown-up, said severely, "Much better. It brings out your bones. And I read that if you have good

59

bones you can be beautiful. Anyhow," she added naïvely, "I like it."

It wasn't till then that their father noticed that there was some actual change in Linda's make-up. "Oh well," he said, when they pointed it out with glee and teased him about his blindness, *"I* see only the essentials."

CHAPTER FOUR

BALANCING a heavy tray, Linda looked around the crowded cafeteria for an empty seat. Rain poured down the windows outside; but here it was steamy and warm, noisy with voices and laughter. *There* was a place—

"Are you saving this for anyone?" Linda asked diffidently. Everyone seemed always to have his own group around him, even here.

"No," the girl responded. "Sit down—if you can manage it." She moved her own chair a trifle, and pushed silverware out of the way. "You're so thin, though, that it won't be difficult." She herself was on the tubby side, with a round face and querulous brows and mouse-colored hair. "You're Linda Marsh, aren't you?" the girl asked as Linda sank gratefully into the narrow space.

The boy on her left did not turn.

"Yes," Linda said, surprised. "How did you know?"

"I'm in a couple of your classes—history and Spanish. I'm Helen Walters."

Linda said, in an embarrassed manner, "Oh . . . Oh, I know I've seen you; but I didn't remember—"

Helen said airily, "Never mind. Nobody ever notices

me . . . at first." There was something a little tart in her way of saying it, although the words were good-natured enough. "I'm used to that. But they will—some-day."

Linda didn't know quite how to answer that. "I'm sure they will," she said at last. "When you're new here—"

"I'm not new. I've been here since Freshman year." The tartness was more apparent now. "Haven't you noticed, though, that there are just a couple of crowds, and they're so snooty they can't see anybody else?"

"Well . . ." Linda said slowly. It was what she had been thinking—that the tight little groups of people she liked and admired from a distance were well satisfied with their members and weren't looking further—but somehow it shocked her to hear it put so baldly. "I—I don't know," she said. "I guess they're all pretty well acquainted."

"It isn't that," Helen retorted. "You're a good student, aren't you?"

Linda was taken aback. "I—I suppose so. I manage to keep up, anyway."

"You're definitely good," Helen said firmly. "I know. So am I. And that"—she leaned forward earnestly—"is why we're not *in*. I could tell you a lot. It's the same old stuff. Jealousy. They don't want people in their crowd who'd shine out or make them seem inferior or anything like that. Personally, I'm just as glad not to be with some of them. I pick my own friends."

Linda bit reflectively into a sandwich. That might be

62

an explanation, of course. Still, there was Ben Brixton and Jimmy Post and Carol Burroughs—they were all tops in their work. Carol was across the hall now, dominating a table for eight. She watched the vivid, animated face of the tall, handsome girl with a sort of wistful envy. She seemed to have everything—just everything.

"Tell me about Carol Burroughs," she said suddenly.

Helen laughed. "So you've fallen for her, too? Everybody does, of course. At first. And the others stick around for what they can get out of her."

"How do you mean?"

"Well, you know, don't you, that her family's one of the richest in town? Her father's head of Burroughs Company—they make presses, and the war boom hasn't done anything to make them poorer! Her mother's a social leader—such as this town has—and she gives swell parties for Carol. Oh, believe me, Carol's going to be launched early. *And* right. It's not enough to belong to one of the First Families of Brookhaven—she's having just a certain crowd built up around her. They're always small parties. Supposed to be exclusive, or something. I've never been; but to hear some people talk who *have* been, you'd think they'd been invited to court. Crazy!" Her nose wrinkled disdainfully. "Just because someone has wealth doesn't make her the best person in town . . . though you'd think so the way some of the kids act, fawning on her to get invited and kowtowing around and being yeswomen all over the place—"

63

"She seems popular," Linda ventured. "I always thought she was terribly attractive."

"Has she spoken to you?"

"N-no."

"Exactly," Helen Walters said triumphantly. "Has any of her set done more than nod to you, offhand, when they happened to think of it? No. That's the way they are. Personally, I think good manners are more important than—than dollars, and I have different standards."

Some of Helen Walters' words went home. *Had* any of them done more than nod to her, or throw her a casual word when it was unavoidable? Take Ben, for instance. She had thought, after that encounter on the street when he had noticed her new hair-do and said she looked swell, that things would be different; that he'd know her now . . . be one of the first to draw her into a widening group. But it hadn't worked out that way. Oh, he spoke, of course—in class, in the hallways—but she might have been anybody. He went his own way, busy, popular, prominent . . . and she continued to be an unimportant cog in the machinery. Not even a recognized cog. It hurt; more than that, it rankled.

"Where do you come from?" Helen Walters' question brought her up sharply.

"Why, I'm from Wayneville."

"That's western New York state, isn't it?"

Linda nodded. "Do you know it?"

"No. I just like to guess where people are from. I placed you right away as western New York state—from your accent. It's a sort of game with me," she explained. "I'm quite good at it. . . . By the way, are you going to class elections this afternoon?"

"I don't know."

There was no reason to hurry home now. But there was no reason to stay, either.

"It's a foregone affair; not much use turning up. Ben Brixton will be president again. Jim, secretary. La Burroughs, vice president. I could name the whole slate and win a bet on it. It's all cut and dried. That's what I hate. Never a chance for anybody who isn't part of the gang's setup."

"Aren't they good?" Linda asked diffidently.

"Oh—good, yes, if you don't mind being bossed by the same old crew year after year. They run the show, and it's full of politics. I wouldn't touch it with a ten-foot pole. . . . Listen," she said suddenly, "why don't you and I cut it? I can see you'd be just as fed up with the way things are run as I am. Come over to my house. I'd love to have you. I feel somehow that we've got a lot in common, if we get acquainted. Do you play badminton?"

"Not very well."

"Neither do I. But we could bat some balls around. And I'll give you the low-down on some goings on here. What's more, I've an idea. I'd like to tell you— Oh, there's the bell! Listen, I'll see you end of history class, shall I? It's been grand meeting you. I know we're going on from here."

The tubby figure gave her a beaming smile, a pat on

the shoulder, and was gone. Linda sat where she was, till second bell roused her to action. Well, at least she'd made a start. There was someone who had seen her, liked her, made an effort to speak to her, and wanted to begin a friendship. She had ideas, too. Linda thought. "I suppose I *can* find out a lot. Not that I see eye to eye with her in everything, but I suppose she knows a good deal that I don't; she's been here so much longer." It wouldn't hurt to have the "low-down" on some things. She decided to go over to Helen's after school. She was hungry for companionship.

On her way out of the cafeteria, Ben Brixton hailed her. She was so startled that she wheeled suddenly and almost ran into him.

"Hi, there! I'm scouting for class meeting this afternoon. You're turning up, aren't you?"

"I—well, I don't know—"

"Sure you are. Class spirit demands it," he said with exaggerated severity. "Haven't you any class spirit for dear old forty-four?"

"Not very much," she admitted, with a small grin. "I haven't had time to get it."

"Well, you turn up and we'll fill you full of it. I mean it. There are going to be big doings, and we need everybody's help." He flashed her a sudden smile. "You'll come, won't you?"

She wanted to tell him how glad she was that at last she was noticed, was needed . . . if only for a class meeting. She wanted to tell him that this meant something more to her than he could imagine; it marked a turning point.

But perversely she said, "I've got a date."

"Break it."

"Do you believe in doing that?"

"Only on special occasions. Like this."

"Well, of course . . . I don't see how I could avoid turning up now. It's practically orders, it seems."

"That's right! Orders it is. And if you aren't there at five past three, we'll send the armed forces out after you."

Helen Walters lingered at the back of the room after History IV. "You're coming?"

"Oh, Helen, I'd love to. In fact, I planned on coming; but Ben Brixton——"

Helen gave her a queer, enigmatic smile. "Don't tell me. He cornered you in the hall, turned on the famous charm-smile, and asked you to be sure and come to class election. Am I right?"

Linda flushed. "Well——"

"Go ahead. I know how it is. But don't say I didn't warn you. You'll be bored to death."

"He made it sound important; and of course I know I ought to go, at least once——"

"Oh, sure!" Helen said airily. "Go on and find out. You won't get a chance to open your mouth; the same old crowd will go in again. And all Ben Brixton wanted out of you was a vote. He's wonderful at getting out the vote. . . . Talk about politics!"

Linda felt chilled. Maybe that was true. It had the

possibility of truth behind it; Helen claimed to know, from experience, what she was talking about. And Ben *hadn't* spoken to her at any length until now . . . when it was probably vital to him to have a big majority.

"Well," she said hesitantly, "all I can do is go and see. I'm really sorry about this afternoon, Helen. I hadn't promised, of course, but I had hoped to go with you. Maybe some other time?"

"Why not? We'll just put it off a couple of days. How about Friday? And no fooling; no turning me down for any class presidents or track stars or such."

Linda laughed. "I won't stay away even if Mr. Galbraith asks me!"

Helen grinned. "You might have to then. . . . Well, so long. I hope you're cured by four o'clock. See you tomorrow."

Linda went to class meeting with mixed feelings. Helen had been disappointed in her, she knew that; but she'd taken it pretty well. And she'd make up to her tomorrow for having turned her down today. Probably Helen was disgusted with her for falling for Ben Brixton's "line," his political friendliness. She must have seen him work it often on others, and was distressed that Linda had succumbed so promptly. It *was* a little queer. Still, she'd go with an open mind. The class election wasn't everything. He'd spoken of "big doings." Maybe she could fit into some of them, even in a small way. She hurried her steps. It would be a grand way of getting to know people; she

68

would show them, too, what she could do, once she had the chance.

The air in the cafeteria, which had been cleared of its tables and had rows of chairs substituted, was electric with excitement. Knots of earnest boys and girls huddled in corners, met and harangued, parted with "You know what I mean!" and "Don't forget, now!" flung over their shoulders.

Carol Burroughs spotted her making her way to a chair. "So glad you came!" she smiled brilliantly. "We're having a swell representation!"

Linda sat down near the back. She returned a nod here and there, but no one she knew was near her. The meeting began promptly, and was conducted with businesslike formality. "The chair asks—" "Is there a motion?" . . . "May we have the report of the nominating committee?"

Elmer Freeman, a tall, gangling lad with a bass voice, got up and boomed, "For president, Benjamin Brixton. For first vice president, Carol Burroughs. For second vice president, Samuel Hellburn. For secretary, James Post. For treasurer, Gene Trumbull. Respectfully submitted—"

There were cheers, which the chair promptly silenced. "You have heard the report of the nominating committee. Are there any nominations from the floor?"

Silence. Then someone got up and said quickly, "I move that the nominations be closed."

"All in favor—"

A roar of "Ayes!" vociferous and gay.

"Those opposed—"

There was no opposition.

Linda was stupefied with amazement. It was exactly as Helen had said. Cut and dried. Made to order. The same crew in again.

Ben Brixton took the chair amid loud applause. "Thanks," he said. "Well, you've put me in again and I hope you won't be sorry. I had a grand bunch working with me last year and they were so well trained that I'm glad I don't have to part with them. I guess you know what you were doing, putting us all to work for you again. Anyhow, we appreciate the compliment. And, believe me, if you think that's all you had to do—to put us back to work for you—you're due for a big jolt. We're in to make *you* work. What's more, you're going to like it. Last year we went to war. This year we're *in* the war—up to our necks, and with all our hearts. We're out to win, and it's a deadly serious business. Some of our friends are in the service. Some of our girls are working. Those of us who're still here—and we don't know how long we'll be here—have to make every minute count. We've got to go places in the little time that's left to us.

"That's why I say you'll all have to work. Nobody's going to escape. Anyhow, I don't think any of you want to escape. We're not working for ourselves this year, or just for our class, or for our school; we're in a bigger play, and we're going to have a smash curtain. There's a

70

place for every one of us. It'll be up to the committees to find that place. If any of you have ideas about yourselves, or others, let me know. I'll always lend an ear; we can always use plenty of ideas."

Linda found herself cheering with the rest. A surge of excitement swept through her. He knew how to rally people to his side! There was to be room for her—for everyone who wanted to take part in this wartime school life.

"In a couple of weeks," Ben was saying, "we'll have things planned out somewhat. There will be committees appointed, and we'll try to work everybody in. All I want to say now is: Watch the fur fly when we get started, and be prepared to shed your shirt when the word comes around!"

Linda would have liked to go up to Ben right after the meeting and tell him how inspiring he'd been, that she was ready to do whatever was demanded of her. But he was surrounded by an enthusiastic group of well-wishers and friends, and the place was bedlam.

Carol Burroughs, near the door, saw her on the way out.

"I'm glad you were elected," Linda said shyly, and Carol smiled.

"Thanks a lot. It was grand of you to come."

Then she, too, was lost in the crowd.

A knot of people in the corridor moved slightly to let her pass. "Doesn't it gripe you?" someone was muttering.

"Same old tripe—same old soap. I'll bet he doesn't even know we exist when he gets 'organized.' " There was immeasurable scorn in the words.

"Yeah, and another thing—what chance has our bunch when *they* are so well organized in the first place that they can put in whom they want and put over whatever they want?"

" 'Are there any nominations from the floor?' " another mimicked bitterly. "And who had a chance to let out a peep? And what would have happened if he *had* let out a peep?"

But, Linda thought, if they were so dissatisfied, why hadn't they spoken out? She remembered the utter silence when nominations were asked for, when "contrary" was voted. And the election had apparently been unanimous. Hadn't these malcontents voted at all? Or was it only after the meeting that they realized they had lost their chance to register disapproval?

She recalled, with a faint sense of guilt, how she herself had been swept along on the current of loud enthusiasm. She had voted for the straight ticket herself; Helen Walters' prophecy was true enough. But Linda honestly admired all the people on the slate. What if it was cut and dried? They were all good material. She certainly couldn't imagine any better. And if others could, why hadn't they spoken out?

Walking home, she decided that she would volunteer for any activity where she was needed. She could hardly wait for the various projects to be listed so she could make a choice. Probably she would be approached long before that and asked to fill a quota of workers in some field or other. She was a good worker; and this war was certainly something into which you could fling all your energy, knowing what a tremendous cause was at stake.

She expected, somehow, to find the school buzzing with the idea next day, but things seemed about as usual. They had lost some of the first fine frenzy; that was natural. But when the time came for action it wouldn't be hard to whip them into line again.

Between classes she found herself minus a handkerchief and went into the locker room to get one out of her coat pocket. The key refused to turn in the lock, and she was fumbling impatiently with it when she heard two girls talking behind the solid line of lockers.

They were discussing someone with a good deal of heat, pulling her to pieces. Linda suspended operations and listened. She was sure she knew their voices—Joan Daniels and Dana Goodwin. They were always with the Carol Burroughs crowd.

"Oh, she's not bad-looking, though I could see room for improvement. It's the way she speaks. She positively *whines!*" Yes, that was Joan talking.

Linda felt vaguely uncomfortable. Her father had often told her not to whine so, but of course that was purely a parental trait—parents always wanted you to be somewhat different from the way you were.

"Somebody ought to tell her," Dana suggested.

73

"Somebody ought, yes. But who? Would you volunteer? *I* wouldn't stick my head into it for any price."

"Even her best friend won't tell her."

Joan laughed. "Maybe she hasn't any, with that voice. Anyhow, even if we were willing to have our hands slapped for our trouble, nobody knows her well enough. They just moved here this summer, I think. From somewhere up in New York state."

"Heavens, if that's a sample of New York state twang I'll stay in New Jersey."

"It has its points."

They drifted away. Linda stood rooted to the spot. Waves of mortification swept over her, hot and nauseating. For it *was* she they were talking about. At first she couldn't believe it, but their words left no doubt. And the scorn in their voices, talking about *her* voice!

Was it as bad as that? Was that why she'd been ignored, left out? Oh, it couldn't be! Why, her father would have told her— But he *had* told her. She ought to try to correct it, he had said; she ought to remember. . . . His words had served only to annoy her and had drifted in one ear and out the other. Now, all the constant little admonitions, so tiresome and frequent, came rushing back in a damning flood. And Bob's teasing way of mimicking her. Calling her Old Whiny-Voice!

She felt stiff with bewildered surprise. A bell rang sharply in the corridor. Next class . . . English. She wouldn't go. She couldn't open her mouth; she couldn't face a roomful of people who, she knew now, were critical

74

and condemning. She'd go home. She wouldn't come back to this miserable old school. She hated the place; she hated Brookhaven; she hated everybody in it!

Setting themselves up like little gods. Criticizing *her* way of speaking. Were they all so perfect, so marvelous? She could think of a dozen people whose voices she didn't like, who were slovenly in their speech. And George Hanson swallowed half his last syllables; Myra Janway had a lisp; Cecile Cummings dropped her *r*'s and attached *r*'s to all words ending in *a*. . . . She could go on and on. Did they think they had a right to criticize her because she had a twang . . . no, because she *whined?* It was a hateful word; it sounded as if the person who did it was crabbed and old and practically toothless. You said a beggar whined. A child crying for the moon. Someone who had done wrong and was afraid of consequences.

And they applied it to her. Did they judge her, then, just by her voice? Because she whined (oh, she couldn't bear that word!) did they think she had a mean, small character? Was *that* how they sized her up? Was that— she shuddered a little—why they hadn't made any advances so far, treating her merely as a member of the class whom they had in their midst but whom they were under no obligation to take *into* their midst?

Second bell. She'd be late for class. "But I'm not going," she thought defiantly.

And then she was ashamed of herself. "I'm a coward, running away from an unpleasant truth. . . . If it *is* a truth. I won't believe it, entirely." She *had* to go to class

. . . just to show them that she didn't care. When she cared so terribly.

She forced her unwilling feet along the endless corridors. It was one of the hardest things she had ever done to turn in at English III, where everyone sat waiting.

"You're late, Linda," Miss Kittredge said crisply.

Those who hadn't turned to look at her before, looked now. She felt thirty pairs of eyes moving over her. In a panic of embarrassment she slid into her seat. Two of her books toppled with an unseemly thud to the floor. Somebody snickered. Miss Kittredge waited patiently while Linda retrieved them, coming up with her face scarlet and her hair hanging in her eyes.

"You all know the saying, 'The last shall be first,' " Miss Kittredge said, almost too pleasantly. "Suppose, then, we start with you, Linda. Tell us your impression of Mr. Churchill's collection of speeches, please."

Oh glory, she had forgotten that Thursdays were Oral Book Reviews! She was prepared well enough—in fact, she had prepared so far in advance that she had practically forgotten what she had intended to say. But that it should be today of all days when she was called upon to get up and speak for three minutes before the whole class! "I can't go through with it," she thought in an agony of mortification. "I just can't, that's all. I'll tell her I have a bad headache; my throat's sore. I'll tell her—"

She found herself automatically getting to her feet. The thirty pairs of eyes were all focused on her, needle-sharp. "I think—" she began painfully. How did that sound? Whiny? Did the *n* twang too much? How could she help its twanging? How did you *keep* your voice from sounding the way it did?

"Well," said Miss Kittredge dryly, "I'm sure it will be interesting if you get around to it."

Linda realized that she had been standing there, blank and silent. She swallowed hard. "I think—that is, Mr. Churchill—is a man—a man—"

Somebody laughed.

Miss Kittredge said severely, "There's nothing humorous about that. We'll all grant that he is a man. Do proceed."

"I mean—" Oh, how full of *n*'s the English language was! Trying to avoid more of them, she stuttered, "He thinks what he says—that is, he says what he thinks. And he says it clearly and beautifully. You know what he means, and at the same time—"

"It seems to be an art that eludes you this morning," Miss Kittredge observed.

Laughter burst in cruel gusts over the room.

"He's a great man. You feel it," Linda plodded on, furious and ashamed. To her ears, suddenly acute, her voice sounded horrible—squeaky and uncertain and nasal. And she was so aware of the critical audience surrounding her that she could not collect her thoughts. "What I mean is—" If there was one thing Miss Kittredge disliked above another, she knew, it was for one of them to keep

77

explaining what he meant. "What I mean is," she heard herself repeating, to her own horror, "is that his greatness is so great—that is, he's such a big man—"

Guffaws broke out again, and the girls twittered.

"He's big. . . . I mean, his character and his insight were marvelous into coming events, so that what he says has a special meaning when you read it; and I think he will go down in history not only as a man who made history but as a man who knew how to write what he said."

Linda wilted into her seat and wished she could hide, wished she could cover her ears. The room rocked with laughter. Miss Kittredge waited till it had subsided.

"I wish I might have had a transcription of that speech, Linda," she said, with her mouth quirked into a most unfamiliar humorous line. "It was a masterpiece of its kind, however unintentional. Now, class, how many of you would rush to the library for the book of Mr. Churchill's speeches after hearing Linda's recommendation?" There was a loud silence. "I thought so. . . . It would seem, Linda, that written reviews from you might help an author's sales more, or at least hinder them less, than your oral report. Now, Gwen, let us hear from you."

The period was never-ending. Now they would have something else to talk about. She'd made a prize idiot of herself, a spectacle. She could imagine some of them getting together and imitating her. "I mean"—with an exaggerated twang—"he's a man—I mean—he's so big —that is—" and dissolving into gales of merriment. She'd be the laughingstock of the school. Why had she opened her mouth in the first place? She should never have come to class.

The rest of the day was torture. She avoided the locker room until everyone had left; then she collected her things and rushed home.

Mrs. Parsons hailed her from the kitchen. "Lamb patties, you said, and carrots. And what's for dessert?"

"Anything," Linda said. "Anything. And I'll be busy until dinnertime."

She locked the door to her room and stood in front of the mirror. Her rebellious eyes met their mirrored reflection. "I'll show them!" she muttered, and then watched her mouth moving in fascination. "I'll show them!" It was a vow. She repeated it wildly to herself, aloud, in all kinds of tones.

She fronted the mirror, stretching her mouth, rounding it, moving her tongue forward and back. She practiced a sentence over and over, now high, now low, then still lower. Slowly. Mouthing it, trying to remember how Carol Burroughs spoke, what Gwen Miller sounded like. Not affected . . . but, well, sort of English.

Her eyes glittered with a feverish light and her pulse beat in her temples when she came down to dinner.

Purposely she kept silent until Amy and Bob had exhausted their daily supply of news and views, and her father's attention was more or less free. Then she cleared her throat.

"Fahthah," she said carefully. ("Remember now—

79

keep it low and open.") He looked up sharply. "Fahthah, will you please pahss the buttah?"

Amy dropped her spoon. Bob sputtered into his soup, "Jeepers, what's the matter with *you?*"

"I ahsked foah the buttah. Is thaht so—ah, unusual?" Linda said, her color rising beetlike to stain her forehead.

"She's sick, Pop," Bob said. "Migosh, what's she coming down with? 'The but-tah, I ahsk you!'" he whinnied. He pressed a napkin over his face.

Mr. Marsh said mildly, "Have you turned Anglophile, my dear, or just what is this—a part in a play?"

Linda, unaccountably and to her own surprise, burst into tears and rushed from the room.

CHAPTER FIVE

MRS. PARSONS called, "Don't forget the coffee. And tell that Star store butcher, if you're going there, that the bacon he sent was too fat!"

Linda said, "I'll choose it myself this time," and escaped.

It was a beautiful morning—sunny and golden, with an intense autumn blue sky overhead. Leaves swirled in bright gusts down the street before her, and there was a smoky tang in the air. It was invigorating weather—weather for long hikes, for football games, for corn roasts. There were a dozen things that she would have liked to do, and that others were doing. Only she was not included. And there was no fun doing them alone.

Even Saturday-morning shopping, necessary and unavoidable as it was, might have been fun if she could have gone arm in arm with some friend . . . talked over school with her, planned a date for Sunday, called careless greetings to chums they passed. That would have made a lark of a chore. Now it was only a chore.

The shopping center was bustling and gay. Women exchanging gossip in front of their cars. Children, let loose among the fruits and vegetables while their mothers ordered, bumping their shins on baskets and sampling grapes surreptitiously. Harassed clerks running about. Phones ringing.

Linda pursued her way among the shops, checking off items on her list and leaving the Star store for last. She felt old and settled, like a middle-aged woman buying supplies for her family. "I might as well be," she thought rebelliously. Her father was gone for the day; Amy and Bob were off on exciting dates of their own. Even Mrs. Parsons had set her hair in curlers last night preparatory to an afternoon at the movies with her sister-in-law. "And all I have to look forward to," Linda said to herself, feeling gloomier and more injured than ever, "is a nice long afternoon with a good book, or raking leaves . . . by myself. Ugh!"

The Star store was the busiest of all. Bargains shouted at her from big placards; vegetable bins overflowed with their bright offerings. Linda threaded her way among the customers to the meat counter. She'd have to wait in line, she saw. The butchers were all occupied.

Someone bumped into her, as she studied her list, and said, "Oh, I'm sorry. . . . Why, it's you!"

Linda looked up, her heart thudding unfamiliarly. It was Carol.

"Hello, Carol," she said, trying to sound casual. She thought frantically for something else to say. "Do you— that is, are you doing the family shopping, too?"

Carol made a little face. "And how I hate it! I'm like a duck out of water. Do *you* know what to order?"

Linda said, "Well, I have to. It's an old story to me."

"You mean you do it all the time?"

Linda nodded. "Ever since Mother died . . . and before that, when she was ill," she admitted bravely.

"Well, but what *do* you order?" Carol demanded. "Meats simply get me down. I can't think of a thing. Mother's gone to Cleveland, you see," she explained, running her hand over her long bob, "because my aunt is ill. I thought it was just going to be for a few days and I said, Oh yes, I'd look after everything—the buying and things like that. Then we got word that she'd have to stay at least a month . . . and, my dear, I'm at my wit's end. We had a marvelous cook who used to have ideas of her own; but she's left for a defense job and the supply's no good, but I'm afraid to get rid of her because we might get someone worse. She doesn't have a single thought about what to have for a meal—just throws out her hands and says, 'What you like. I cook what you like.'" Carol gave her low, infectious laugh. "Awfully obliging of her; but I wish she'd up and say, 'Bring home a pound of liver,' or—or something. *I* don't know. I've fed the family on steaks and chops for ten days and they're positively insulting."

Linda couldn't help laughing.

Carol said, with a rueful grin, "That's all very well, perhaps, to you. But does an animal have more—more

83

parts than steaks and chops? I never can seem to think of anything, and those charts"—she waved her hands to a large, segmented picture of a beef creature hanging on the wall—"look so scientific. I don't know a plate from a brisket. And what do you do with them when you've got them?"

"You cook them—how long depends on which cut you get," Linda replied. "Some of the cheaper meats, so called, take longer cooking, of course; but they're just as good. There are all kinds of things you can do with them." She felt queerly excited. Carol Burroughs asking her advice! Carol—coming to *her* for help!

They were moving slowly up the counter.

"Yes, miss?" one of the butchers said briskly. Then, "Well, which one comes first?"

"You go ahead," Linda gave Carol a little shove.

"No, no, you were really first. Besides, I haven't made up my mind yet."

"Well . . ." Linda assented. To the butcher she said, in a businesslike manner, "I'd like a four-pound pot roast, please."

"From the brisket or the bottom round?"

"The bottom round," she answered, without hesitation. "And I'd like a piece of suet, too." The butcher got out a slab of meat and held it up for her inspection. Linda said critically, "That looks very long-fibered. Haven't you something better?"

When the butcher had gone to the refrigerator Carol

said, in awe, "They never do that to me! And I wouldn't know what to say if they did."

"Anything else?" he asked, wrapping the roast in white paper.

"A half pound of bacon, please. Sliced very thin. The last you sent, by the way, wasn't what I ordered. You know I always want it quite fat, with only a few streaks of lean; but that was positively all fat."

"Must have been Joe who sent out your order," the butcher said seriously. "Me, I know the kind you like." He reached into the case. "Like this, huh?"

"That's it. And I want a shoulder of lamb, too. Will you take out the bone, please, and chop it?"

"Sure." He worked busily for a while. "That'll be three-seventy-nine. Next!"

Carol swallowed hurriedly. Linda began picking up the heavy packages.

"Wait!" Carol said in an urgent voice. "Wait. . . . I'd like the same thing," she said to the butcher, while Linda stared at her agape. "Exactly the same . . . four pounds of—uh, round roast; I mean, round pot roast—that is, pot roast from the round." Linda gulped back her laughter, and heard Carol continuing, "And a piece of suet. And will you remove the bone and chop it?"

"The suet?" the butcher asked suspiciously.

"No, the pot roast."

"You mean the shoulder of lamb, Carol," Linda put in.

"Oh, yes, of course! And some bacon—not too lean.

85

What do I do with the chopped bone, anyhow?" she wheeled on Linda to ask.

"You use it for soup, or the stock pot."

"That'll be three-ninety-eight," the butcher said finally.

Carol cried, "But I ordered exactly the same as Miss Marsh and her bill was three-seventy-nine."

The butcher smiled in a tolerant fashion. "Could be I gave you a mite more meat on the pot roast," he said. "Can't cut things off within an eighth of a pound always. You got some over the four pounds."

"Have you got your car outside?" Carol asked.

"We don't have a car," Linda said.

"Well, you're not going to carry all those bundles, are you?"

"I was too late for the morning delivery, so I thought I'd take them along."

"You come with me. Ernest's waiting somewhere down the street. . . . Oh, there he is!"

A thin, slightly stooped man with a lined face and wearing a chauffeur's uniform had appeared in the doorway and now came forward to relieve them of their bundles. "I'm parked on South Street, Miss Carol," he said.

"I'll take you home," Carol offered. "You'd be bent over with a load like that. Besides, you've got to tell me what to tell Agnes about the lamb shoulder." Ernest stowed them in the back seat of the shiny black sedan, and put their bundles in the trunk compartment. "We'll take Miss Marsh home first, Ernest," Carol said. She turned to Linda. "I'm sorry, I—I don't know where you live."

"We're on Tremont. We took the Griscom house."

"Oh, I know! That sweet place with the blue shutters!"

It was fun, riding in the smooth-running car, telling an interested Carol about stuffing a shoulder of lamb and how to use the leftover meat for fricandels.

"I think you're wonderful!" Carol cried wholeheartedly. "I feel so *dumb!* I don't suppose you could help me out, too, with some easy desserts? Agnes can't tackle anything complicated, and everything I think of seems to be beyond her."

"Oh yes, I know lots of them," Linda said eagerly. "Desserts are my specialty. I'm crazy about them, and I'm always looking up recipes and trying them out. They *have* to be easy, because I don't have the time to spend on any other kind. I know a wonderful lemon marlo, and an apricot betty that melts in your mouth, and some perfectly grand cranberry tarts that are simple to make."

"You're going to save my life; I can see that," Carol said, her mouth curving in a generous smile. "I'm so glad I bumped into you!"

"If you'll wait, I'll copy the recipes for you. It won't take a minute."

"I won't stir without them. Just wait till I spring stuffed shoulder of lamb and lemon marlo on my long-suffering family . . . provided Agnes can get the hang of them."

Ernest leaped out and opened the car door, and carried Linda's packages up to the door. Mrs. Parsons was dusting in the living room, her head tied up in a towel. Her mouth dropped slightly when she saw Linda's approach, but she hurried to take the bundles from Ernest and held open the screen door.

"What a charming house!" Carol said warmly, her eyes taking in the sunny room with its fresh flowers and chintzes. "I used to know the Griscoms. . . . You've done something to this room, haven't you? I don't remember that it seemed so big."

Linda swelled with pride. It had been Mrs. Clayborne's guidance, but it was *her* house. Praise from someone like Carol Burroughs meant something.

"It's the light walls and furniture," she said modestly, "and having curtains only at the sides, I think. Sit down, Carol, while I get the cards from my file box."

Mrs. Parsons said, *sotto voce,* "My, you *are* elegant, riding home from market in a see-dan and with a chauffeur to carry your packages. Is she staying to lunch, for goodness' sake, and what'll I have?"

"No . . . that is, I haven't asked her yet," Linda said, struck with a new idea. "I'll let you know."

She hurried back and opened up the desk, glad that it was so neat—with all its pigeonholes in order. Carol chattered in a friendly fashion about all kinds of things while she copied. She would have liked it to take a long time . . . it was so pleasant to have Carol Burroughs here, in her house, perched on the edge of the sofa and babbling like an old friend. Carol had such a lovely voice. . . . Suddenly she was horribly conscious of her own. She had forgotten all about it, during this strange morning. She had just talked—unheeding. How had she sounded? What must Carol have thought of her? Had she— whined? Oh dear, if she'd only had more time to practice before she met Carol in this intimate way!

The recipes were all written; she folded the papers slowly. Her throat felt dry and constricted.

"Heah they ah," she said meticulously. ("Keep it low; keep it round and open," she abjured herself solemnly.) Carol stared at her, a sentence bitten off in mid-air. "Would you—that is, I'd love to have you stay for luncheon, Carol. I do so want to know you bettah."

Carol jumped up. "Thanks," she said queerly. "But I'd no idea it was this late! Heavens, I'm due at the dress-maker's this minute!" She held out her hand for the recipes. "Thanks a million, Linda. You've been such a help." She moved toward the door, and Linda, regret-fully, moved with her. "I'll be seeing you!"

In a twinkling she was gone. Linda stared out at the disappearing car through eyes that blurred swiftly. It was like a dream . . . meeting Carol, the gay talk, having her here in the house— And now it was over. "I'll be seeing you." That might mean anything. And possibly nothing. She remembered Carol's odd look of astonish-ment when she had begun to speak with her new voice. It was then she had said she couldn't stay. What had been wrong?

Maybe she was inventing things; maybe she was exag-gerating what had happened.

Mrs. Parsons came in with a tray with two glasses of cider. "I thought you'd like a drink—"

"She's gone," Linda said flatly. "She had an appointment."

"Oh well," said Mrs. Parsons philosophically, "maybe you can drink both of them. Or Master Bob will when he comes in. . . . I'm just as glad she didn't stay. I was going to have all leftovers for lunch, anyhow, and I want to get away early."

"But it would have been lovely if she could have stayed," Linda thought wistfully. The beginning of everything she longed for. No one had been to visit her—except Mrs. Clayborne, and that was different, somehow. Not like a girl her own age. Oh, Helen, of course. But—well, Helen was different, too.

Perhaps Carol really had had to get to the dressmaker's. Perhaps meeting up with Linda, and getting the recipes, wasn't anything out of the ordinary to her. Linda thought, "I have to remember that. She's used to seeing people all the time, being welcome, having things done for her." And she had said, "I'll be seeing you." That was what everybody said. How could she set a date? She was busy—she'd said herself that taking charge of the house was a new kind of job for her and kept her occupied. She'd see her at school, anyhow . . . they'd be on a different footing now. Not just classmates who nodded to each other in passing. They were on a more intimate basis. It could be the beginning—

Resolutely Linda clung to that, because she wanted to

90

believe it so desperately. Her voice, and the sudden change, might have had something to do with Carol's refusal and her abrupt departure. But then it might not. The voice was a matter that had to be tended to, anyhow. She wasn't going to be downed by her brother's and Amy's ridicule. Her father believed in her, at least. He had come to her room, after that sudden flight from the dinner table that she was ashamed of now, and had said gently, stroking her hair, "You've made a start in the right direction, Lin. It's always hard at first. You mustn't be so easily discouraged. Young people, you know—" He had made her feel grown-up with him, smiling tolerantly at the intolerance of the young. Amy and Bob had heard only the result; her father sensed the reason, and the effort behind it.

Amy had said, "You sound like somebody with throat trouble," and Bob had simpered affectedly, in an uncomfortable imitation of her attempt. But her father had said, "You'll get it. Just try to keep it natural-sounding, Lin."

Natural-sounding! It was easy to advise. But how did you, when your natural voice was branded as a whine?

She needed help. But where was she to get it? She was too proud to ask Mrs. Clayborne for help in this, too. Besides, it was such a personal matter. If she could battle it out by herself . . .

After Mrs. Parsons had departed, every wave in place, she remembered her prospect of spending the afternoon alone with a "good book." Why couldn't the good book be something on voice training? Could you get help from a book on voice training? She didn't know . . . it hardly seemed possible, but it was worth trying.

Mrs. Clayborne willingly signed her application at the Public Library, and she walked back with the signed card and asked the attendant for a book on voice training.

"Something—something you could study at home," she said painfully.

It was a slim book that she carried out. But meaty, she discovered. Notes to practice. Diagrams. A description of the throat muscles and resonant cavities. Sentences to say over and over. How to shape her mouth.

It was fascinating, once you got into it. She was glad everyone was out. In front of her bedroom mirror she sang, "La-la-la-la, mimimimi." She placed her hand on her chest and said slowly, "Ninety-nine. Nine hundred and ninety-nine," trying to feel the proper vibrations that the book said should be there.

"The King of England doth approach!" she proclaimed majestically. "Open the gates! The King of England doth approach!"

That struck her funny, suddenly. What would she do if the King *did* approach? She doffed an imaginary cape and bent low, sweeping it in a magnificent arc of homage. . . . And what good would it do her to say this with the proper roundness and intonation? Could she go up to the butcher and demand, "Open the gates! The King of England doth approach?" Better to try saying, "A half pound of your best bacon, please, and not too much lean." Why, there were quite a few *n*'s in that! Try it again. "A half pound of your best bacon, please. And not too much lean."

The afternoon passed magically. Mrs. Parsons' voice startled her.

"Did you call me?"

"Mercy, I didn't even realize you were home!"

"I heard a voice. You got company?"

"No," Linda said, with what dignity she could muster, "I was talking to myself."

Mrs. Parsons came up the stairs at that. "You been here all afternoon by yourself?"

"Yes—"

"You ought to go out more," Mrs. Parsons said severely. "When you get to talking to yourself, it's time to go out more."

At school on Monday, Helen Walters came up and thrust her arm through Linda's. "I saw you coming out of the library Saturday, when I was halfway across the park, and I yelled my head off and ran after you; but you had your nose in a book and didn't even hear me—I guess."

"No, I didn't, Helen. I'm sorry."

"Must have been an awfully interesting book. What was it?"

Linda felt her face flushing. She wasn't ready to be questioned, or to be criticized, either, for that matter.

Helen saw the flush and misinterpreted it. "Don't tell me!" she said with a sly smile. "We all read 'em when

93

we get the chance. A change from Mr. Churchill's speeches, anyhow."

Linda saw Carol then and her heart bounded. Would Carol say—

"Hi, Linda! The family said to tell you the apricot betty was swell, and as for the stuffed lamb—" She made an eloquent gesture. "You were a lamb yourself to give it to me."

"But not stuffed," Linda managed, feeling lighthearted and foolish.

Helen turned to her suspiciously. "What is this—some new sort of code?"

In a rush of confidence Linda told her. Helen listened with a satirical quirk to her mouth.

"Well, well, so you fell for it, too! The old gag about needing help, and making you feel all puffed up that you could give it! She's a whiz at getting things out of people—sweet as pie until she has what she wants."

"But she said—" Linda began indignantly.

"I know," Helen said impatiently. "I've heard it used over and over. It never fails, I must hand it to her. But I thought you— Well," she said magnanimously, "of course you're new here." Suddenly she squeezed Linda's arm. "You poor thing! I'll bet you thought it was going to be the beginning of a bee-ootiful friendship, didn't you? Admittance to the select Burroughs circle!"

"I don't see why you say that," Linda muttered, but underneath she was bothered by it.

That was just what she had thought. Was she that naïve?

"You will—in time," Helen prophesied. "It takes time for some things to sink in. Especially with people like you," she said cryptically. "Just wait. Tell me later whether she goes on from there. Or asks you to her house. Or draws you into her crowd. Just tell me—say, in a couple of weeks."

"I was glad to help her if I could," Linda said stiffly, salvaging her pride.

"Sure, sure!" Helen concurred. "You used to be a Girl Scout, and the training sticks. I never was one. That's why I can see through people like La Burroughs."

Helen was a queer girl. Linda couldn't make up her mind about her. Sometimes she sounded soured on the world; other times, Linda thought, she was simply clear-thinking. She saw matters as they were, not as she would like them to be.

Oddly pricked by Helen's remarks, she waited, with every sense alert, for further developments from Carol. In the meantime the school buzzed with activity; there were plans being worked out, meetings were being held, clubs and work groups formed. Linda felt a mounting sense of excitement . . . in this busy wartime world, bounded though it was by school routine, there would be a place for her. She held back for a while, trying to decide where she would fit and what she would join. She had

95

hoped that someone would approach her—in fact, that she would be approached perhaps by half a dozen groups, each wanting to enlist her aid. When no one spoke to her particularly, she swallowed her pride and her hurt and stayed after school one day to volunteer for the Cannoneers. The Cannoneers were a band of girls who went several afternoons a week to the small local hospital and to institutions near by to prepare cans for salvage, which released the staff for other duties.

"I'm sorry," said the girl who was efficiently taking down names and going over papers, "there was such a rush for that in the beginning that it's full up." Seeing Linda's face, she added, "Maybe they'll form a second group. I can put your name down meanwhile, and let you know if there's an opening. . . . Or you might want to try for something else."

"Well—" Linda said hesitantly, and then, with resolution, "Yes, I will."

She'd try for the Thread and Thimble, a group of girls who made garments for refugees. That, too, was signed up. Plans hadn't yet been made to enlarge it, Miss Pound said, because they had a limited number of machines.

It was almost as bad with two other activities. There wasn't room for her—everyone else had been there before. It was her own fault, in a way, she admitted . . . but then, again, why hadn't they reached out and drawn her in?

She felt oddly deflated and unhappy as she went slowly home. She had set her heart on the Cannoneers or the

Thread and Thimble especially. She didn't know what else she wanted to join. She didn't know how to play chess, and she wasn't interested in stamp collecting. If some of the other groups came and asked her to work with them, of course she would; it would be a way to get in, and then later, if there was an opening somewhere else, she would take it.

But no one came and asked her. No one seemed to be particularly aware of her existence, outside of classes. Her teachers were kind, but she was only one of thirty or forty. She didn't expect to be singled out there. Her work was satisfactory, apparently, and that was all they really asked of her. She knew they weren't aware of her hunger to be part of the school world . . . she held herself stiff and aloof, so that they wouldn't see how bewildered she was.

The bewilderment grew into a kind of anger as the fall season wore on. The world teemed with excitement— war news and war rumors; the shape of things to come, uncertainty and speculation. There was a tenseness in the air, and a quality of electrical suspense at school. Everyone seemed occupied and busy beyond his capacity for each day. Only she was at a loose end, wondering, and waiting, and growing daily more distressed.

Carol *hadn't* asked her to her house. She was gay and friendly when they met; but they didn't meet often, and then only briefly. Linda heard that her mother had returned . . . so there would be no opportunity to help again. Not in that way. And Carol's friends, taking their

97

cue, perhaps, from her, made no special effort to meet her or to know her better.

At class meetings Linda found herself only a vote, never an active, contributing part. She had ideas . . . she wanted to get up and express them; but she felt tongue-tied and awkward when the impulse came over her, and a kind of stage fright held her back. By the time she had steeled herself to a little courage, the meeting would be over.

She seemed to be going around in a kind of vacuum. There was a busy world around her, but she was not part of it. There was a social world around her, too; but she had no part in it, either. There were comradeship and friendship . . . but not for her. Girls and boys paired off for autumn hikes and picnics in the woods. They went to the football games together and cheered themselves hoarse for Brookhaven High, but she was not there.

When the Junior Quiz, "Misinformation, Thank You," was announced, she felt a lift of hope. She was bright enough to be asked to be one of the "experts." She really shone in history, and English was her next best subject . . . in spite of oral reviews, she admitted wryly. She went to the class meeting determined to put herself forward— to volunteer at once if they asked for volunteers, or to speak to someone and say that she was willing to offer herself up as a lamb for the slaughter. It would be fun . . . and she'd be in a kind of spotlight. People would get to know her, aware at last that there was such a person as Linda Marsh in the high school.

Ben announced the Quiz, the plans for selling tickets, the ushers, the lighting crew . . . and the Board of Dummies, as they were to be called. Jimmy and Sam and Buzz Dean and Lillian Travis and Carol and Sue Hapgood and Loring White. . . .

She stumbled out of the meeting, blinking her eyes furiously. Of course it would have been all settled; of course it was all cut and dried!

Helen met her. "Did you get a ticket? We'll go together! It ought to be a laugh—they'll make such fools of themselves; we're in for a good time."

She went with Helen. They sat far forward, watching, listening, snickering to themselves. It *was* funny. And the Board of Dummies made plenty of mistakes. Helen was scornful; and Linda had an angry feeling, realizing how many answers she knew which the Board missed. She wasn't being egotistical; she *knew*.

"Listen," said Helen suddenly, as they got up and stretched and joined the noisy throng milling toward the exits. "I've been wanting to ask you something for quite a time. But we've been watching you, wanting to see if you were our kind. And now we're satisfied."

Linda turned to stare at her. "What is this? You sound awfully mysterious."

"Not mysterious. Just—well, select. Not everyone can join. In fact, there aren't nearly enough who are . . . well, who are the right sort. Who think as we do, and who belong."

"Belong to what?"

"I mean, who have the necessary qualifications to be asked to join. It's the Reform Club."

She paused expectantly, but Linda looked blank.

"I hadn't heard of it. . . . Should I have?"

"Not if you kept your eyes on Burroughs and Brixton and that bunch. We're not part of the school clubs— nothing juvenile like that. We're adult; we're forward-looking. We meet at each other's houses, and we discuss everything—everything that needs reform, starting right here in the school, and how we'll go about it."

"Heavens!" Linda said inadequately. "I don't know—"

"We don't expect you to answer right away. Come and get acquainted. You'll find we sharpen our minds on all kinds of problems . . . and you must admit there's plenty that needs reforming!"

"Ye-es," Linda agreed.

"Take the way the class meetings are run. The way the crowd in power has everything just as it pleases. The—"

"Who belongs?" Linda interrupted.

"People with minds . . . like you and me. People who see through things and want them changed. It's enough to make you sick, the way things are run . . . and we've got to do something about it. You're one to help."

"Does Mr. Galbraith know about it?"

"Of course not," Helen said impatiently, scorn in her voice. "Why should he? We're free, white, and—near enough twenty-one to manage a few things on our own. If we want to have a reform club outside of school, what's

100

to prevent us? He doesn't know about it, so he doesn't disapprove of it. The next meeting's at my house on Monday. Will you come?"

Linda hesitated. It wasn't what she wanted; it wasn't what she had expected. But what she had expected hadn't happened, and what she wanted seemed as far away as ever. She looked across the hall and saw Carol and Everett Gore and Jimmy Post in a laughing group; Ben Brixton was signaling them wildly from the balcony. She caught the shout, "At the Dainty Shoppe. . . . Hay ride." Carol hadn't asked her over; hadn't gone out of her way to be nice to her. It was just as Helen had predicted. She had been unbelieving then. Now she saw that Helen was right. They didn't want her; there wasn't room for her in that group. Maybe in the Reform Club there would be. At least she had been asked to join something—to join because she was the "right kind."

"All right," she said suddenly, "I will."

CHAPTER SIX

AMY withdrew a bit of meat from her plate and held it out to Jinks. Jinks obligingly sat up on his broad little haunches, his tongue hanging out, his eyes fastened on his mistress.

"Look, Daddy! Daddy, look!" Amy cried urgently.

Mr. Marsh said, "I knew he was to be fed table scraps, but I didn't know it was to be scraps at the table."

"Oh, Daddy, I'm not *feeding* him," Amy said reproachfully. "This is to be his reward for the new trick. We've been practicing it all week while you were gone. It's our surprise. Watch now." She laid the juicy bit of meat across Jinks' nose. He rolled his eyes and his eyebrows twitched; but he remained upright, motionless. "One, seven, eleven," sang Amy in an excited monotone, "two, ninety-eight, seventeen . . ." The little dog's paws quivered and he teetered on his hind legs. *"Three!"* she exploded hastily.

There was a lightning snap of the jaws, and the meat had disappeared. Jinks rested on all fours and then, expectation gleaming in his brown eyes, hoisted himself upright again.

"Gosh, that's good!" Bob cried with approval. "That's swell. You'd think he almost knew which number was which, wouldn't you?"

"He does," Amy said in quick defense. "Of course he does. How else do you think he takes the meat only on 'three' and not on some other number? He's a terribly bright dog."

Suddenly her little face crumpled, and they saw with amazement that tears were about to spill over.

"What's the matter, child?" Mr. Marsh asked in concern.

"It's Jinks. He's so bright . . ."

"Well, that's nothing to cry over. You ought to feel like a proud parent."

"I do," she sobbed. "That's the trouble. I love him, and I'd hate to give him up. I'd just die if I had to give him up!"

"But who says you have to give him up?" Mr. Marsh had a moment's fleeting vision of irate neighbors. "Has anyone been complaining? He does bark quite a lot, I've noticed."

Amy sniffed. "That's because he's a watchdog. And he only barks at the laundryman and the postman and the garbage man and the grocery boy and the iceman . . . Well"—she gave a watery smile—"that is a lot, I guess. But I could teach him not to bark at some of them, once he gets to know them. And baby carriages," she added righteously, "and bicycles, and men with bundles like the Salvation Army . . ."

Mr. Marsh laughed. "You've got your hands full, Amy. But that isn't the trouble. Now out with it."

"It's—it's that they need dogs for the war," she said. Her eyes were worried and anxious, fixed on her father's face. "They read us an article about it today at school. All kinds of dogs. Bright ones, like Jinks. Oh, Daddy, I do want to help the war and—and everything. But would I have to give up Jinks?"

"Of course not, my dear," he said soothingly. "I doubt if they want dogs—well, just like Jinks. Wire-haired terriers—"

"Almost," she felt impelled to insert.

Mr. Marsh amended gravely, "Almost wire-haired terriers. They're after bulldogs and afghan hounds and shepherds. Dogs like that. I think Jinks is safe with you."

Linda, with a rush of sympathy, saw the tremendous relief that flooded over Amy's serious little face.

"But if you want to help win the war—and you can't give up Jinks—I think some sort of sacrifice is in order, don't you?" her father asked.

"Oh *yes,* Daddy! What? We'd do anything. Jinks could work, too, maybe."

"Well, he might pull a grocery cart at that." Her father smiled. "But, as for you, why not give up some candy now and then and buy a war stamp? I notice your book isn't filling up very rapidly."

Amy flushed. Candy was her weakness, and most of her allowance went to indulge her sweet tooth.

Now she said, without a moment's hesitation, "I will.
104

I'll do without candy for—well, for a month, anyhow. And see how it goes," she added. "You know, if I had a piece just now and then—maybe every other month—I could go on through the year. Or, anyhow, till the book is filled up."

"Our school is going to have a salvage contest," Bob said importantly. "And our room's going to win."

"That's good! What makes you so confident?"

" 'Cause they made me captain," he said matter-of-factly. "And that means they think I can do it. And I can."

"Tin can?" Mr. Marsh asked with a twinkle.

Bob guffawed. He loved his father's puns. "Oh, boy! Wait till I tell 'em what you said!"

"Spare me. My reputation hangs by a thread now, I'm afraid."

Linda sat silent. Her father was doing war work, important work; Amy was ready to give up her dog, and forego candy; Bob was captaining his class to success—and he would, too. And what was she doing?

It was Mrs. Clayborne who unwittingly gave her a clue. Linda went in one afternoon to find her neighbor frowning over a set of directions and ripping out rows of knitting.

"Don't speak to me!" she abjured sternly. "I'm ready to bite the first person who comes near me. Why I ever took up a complicated piece of business like a turtle-neck sweater I don't know, except that I'm a softie. I can't say No, when it's the better part of valor to admit in the beginning that I'm a dub at this sort of thing."

105

Linda laughed and dropped down at her feet. Expertly she retrieved the tangled ball of wool, wound it neatly, gathered up papers, stowed some loose needles in Mrs. Clayborne's bag, and asked, "What's it all about? Maybe I can help. Anyhow, if it will help you to bite somebody, go ahead. I won't mind."

For answer Mrs. Clayborne leaned forward and mischievously nibbled at Linda's arm. "There. I feel better. Now, if you can please tell me what I'm supposed to do here, maybe I'll return to sanity. 'Pick up from back of neck fourteen stitches from each side, and twenty-four from front of neck—' "

Linda took the knitting from her and scanned it.

"That's easy. I'll fix it." She counted stitches for a moment. "You should have thirty-two here instead of thirty-eight. That's why it looked so lopsided."

"Thank heaven! You're an angel! At least you don't say it's my queer way of knitting." She held up the garment. "I pity the poor creature who wears this. . . . Maybe it will look better blocked. I don't know *why* I go on knitting when I can do so many other things better. But they're simply mad for four hundred sweaters down at the Red Cross, and they practically hog-tie you if you go near the place. I went down to make bandages and they wouldn't let me out until they'd thrust a bundle of wool in my arms. And I *like* to make bandages," she mourned.

"Are they really so desperate?" Linda asked, with a glimmer of hope.

106

"They're frantic. The order came in, and they say they're afraid they have all the available knitters signed up now; and how they're to get four hundred more sweaters—not to mention all the other things like socks and afghan squares and mufflers and helmets—is simply beyond them. Poor Mrs. Wing! She's in a frenzy. She'll die if Brookhaven doesn't come up to its quota."

Linda stood up. "Excuse me, then. I'll go right down and let them thrust a bundle of wool into *my* arms. I love to knit. I went in several times, you know, and each time they were out of wool, so I thought it was a permanent condition."

"Run along," Mrs. Clayborne encouraged her. "Maybe they'll give you *two* bags. You're young and eager . . . and if you're willing they'll probably make you sign up for the whole four hundred."

Mrs. Wing greeted her with pathetic gratefulness. "My dear, every new knitter is like a feather in my cap! Will you take a turtle-neck? . . . Oh, how marvelous!" She stowed hanks of wool in a bag, thrust in directions and label. "If you can get it back by December first . . . in fact, you must get it back by then; we have to get our consignment off by the fifth. And if you know of anyone else . . . Is there anyone else in your family who knits?"

"Not yet," Linda said, with a smile. "I'm hoping to train my sister, and Bob would have to be roped into it, and Father's too busy. . . . Wait, I might get Mrs. Parsons to try her hand!"

107

"Would you?" Mrs. Wing said urgently. "Perhaps you'd like to take the wool along, just in case?"

Linda, having had a moment to think about it, decided she'd better not. "But I'll come back for it if she can do it," she promised.

Mrs. Parsons, approached delicately on the subject, gave an instant decision. "Not sweaters," she said firmly. "I don't like to work with the big, bulky things. I like to make baby outfits. Now if they want socks or bootees or little caps or things . . ." Her face softened. "I dote on working with light wools and pretty colors."

"I'm sure they'd like those, too," Linda said, though she was doubtful. "Only they're in such need of these turtle-necks, and I thought—"

"Baby things," Mrs. Parsons said with finality, "or nothing at all."

Linda knitted as fast as she could to make up for what she felt was Mrs. Parsons' defection, particularly since she had intimated to Mrs. Wing that the housekeeper might be another knitter. Perhaps, if she worked hard enough, she could do two sweaters in the time it ordinarily took to do one, and in that way they wouldn't miss Mrs. Parsons' contribution.

After English III on Monday, Miss Kittredge asked her to stay a moment. "I don't want to make you late for your next class," she said, "but I did want to tell you, privately, how pleased I've been over your voice. What *have* you been doing?"

Linda colored up to the roots of her hair. "I—I'm

108

glad you told me," she said. "I wondered if there was any improvement. I hoped so. Because, you see, I've just been working on it by myself at home—and trying to remember to practice what I learned, in between—and it's hard to know whether you're getting anywhere at all that way. No one has said anything to me until now."

"I've noticed a big improvement; particularly this last week, and I could scarcely believe my ears! Of course," she added hastily, "there's room for betterment still; but you've made a good start, and I admire your trying. I wonder if you'd like to have a part in the play we're putting on for Christmas?" Linda stood, speechless and happy. It couldn't be! "It's only a small part," Miss Kittredge hurried to assure her. "One of the girls dropped out, and I've been casting around in my mind for someone to fill her place. I think you'd do very nicely."

"I'd love it," Linda said happily. "Only I never know what to do with my hands and feet. . . . I suppose you've noticed."

"Most tall people, and growing young people, have that trouble," Miss Kittredge said kindly. "Taking part in the play might help. It's always a good thing to get on a stage if you can . . . and part of the training would be for just that sort of—awkwardness. Shall I tell Miss Higham you'll come to rehearsal? It's at three-fifteen, right after school."

She felt like skipping down the corridor. At last someone had noticed her! At last her efforts to remedy her voice had had results! This was the beginning. The play would introduce her to others; in fact, to the whole school. Perhaps she'd be asked to join the Drama Club. That *would* be something! They were all carefully selected members, and you had to prove that you had real ability before they took you on.

"Don't forget the R. C.," Helen said importantly, seeing her turn into history room.

"Oh—" Linda stopped short. "I don't know how I'll make it, Helen." She told of her new offer.

Helen stretched her mouth into a thin line and her eyes narrowed. She looked quite unpleasant . . . and distinctly displeased.

"Sa-ay," she said with an unnatural drawl, "what is this? Every time I ask you to something at my house, you've got a reason why not."

"Oh, Helen!" Linda was distressed. "You mustn't think that! It's just—things happen to come at the same time, it seems, and—well, like this! When I said I'd come to the club meeting, I had no idea I'd be asked for the play. And I've got to turn up, and I'd have to stay as long as they wanted me to . . . or as long as rehearsal lasts, anyhow. Don't you see?"

"No," Helen said deliberately, "I'm afraid I don't. You knew about the club long before you were asked for this. Anyhow, it seems to me you'd have a little pride. Can't *you* see that you're just being asked because somebody else dropped out?"

Yes, Linda thought miserably, there was that reason. Miss Kittredge had said so. But she had also said—

110

"She also said that it was because my voice had improved a lot," Linda blurted out, smarting under Helen's accusing eye.

"That's a laugh," Helen said rudely. "You still sound like western New York to me. . . . But go ahead. I must say I'm disappointed in you; and I guess the others will be, too. But we asked you, and *we're* not reneging. Come when rehearsal's over. If ever."

And with that she was gone.

Going to rehearsal afterward, Linda felt deflated and unhappy. The episode had bothered her all through history period, and she had difficulty keeping her mind on the work. She could see Helen's side of it. But why couldn't Helen see *her* position? And that crack about her voice still being the same— She wondered whether she ought to try to go to the club at all. It wouldn't be very pleasant now. Helen had seemed ready to wipe her hands of her entirely. And she didn't want to give up Helen . . . she was her only intimate in the whole school.

Linda thought, "I've muffed it again. What did I do wrong? And why can't things come right for me?"

Surprisingly, however, there was a break in her luck. Miss Higham, the dramatic coach, had the cast assembled and rehearsal had already started when Linda appeared. She broke off, while all the cast stared and listened, and told Linda that, since the play was divided into two acts and her part didn't come until the second half, she might as well take her script and study it and then be

111

prepared for rehearsal on Wednesday, when they were going to run through the whole play.

"Not once, but several times, I'm afraid!" Miss Higham said, with laughing sternness. "We've a lot to do on it if we want to put on a decent performance, and I want more than a decent performance—I want a startlingly good one. So everybody be letter-perfect by then, or answer to me for the consequences!"

Linda said timidly, "Didn't you want to—to try me out?"

Miss Higham ran a hand through her short hair. "My dear, I'm taking Miss Kittredge's word for it that you'll do. We're so short on time I am willing to take her word on anybody! Just see that you don't disappoint me. I want you here at every rehearsal after this."

So that's how it was. They were so in need of somebody to fill in that anybody—even Linda Marsh—would do. She took her script and crushed it in her hand.

"I'll go along then," she said with what dignity she could muster, "and I'll know my part by Wednesday. I—I have a date now."

"Go ahead," Miss Higham dismissed her. "I'm sure you'll be all right. . . . Now, Isabel, for the tenth time, let's run through that long speech. And a *little* feeling!"

Near the Music Hall she ran into Everett Gore.

He stopped in mid-career and grabbed her by the arm. "Hey, you look like a recruit! Come on in and raise your voice. We're short a couple of sopranos and altos, and you can take your pick."

"I can't sing," she protested.

"That's what they all say," he answered in a blithe voice, "except those who think they're Lily Ponses. The choir's shaping up nicely, but we need some extras. Dr. Howe will give you a run-through."

"But I can't—really I can't!" she cried. "I just croak."

"The rest will drown you out."

"No, there's no use. I tried out in Wayneville, and it was terrible! Singing's one of the things I can't do. And besides—"

"I know, you have a date!" he mocked. "That's the old excuse, but it's a good one. Whither bound?"

He asked it mostly in fun, she knew, and didn't really rate an answer. But she wanted him to know that she did have a date, and wasn't simply giving him an excuse to get out of trying for the choir.

"I'm due at the Reform Club," she said importantly.

He raised his eyebrows; his face underwent a peculiar change.

"Oh-oh," he said. It might have meant anything . . . but she was afraid it meant disapproval. "So that's your bunch, is it? Well, excuse me for holding you up."

Linda walked slowly to Helen's house, wondering what sort of reception she'd have—or whether she should have gone at all. Helen met her at the door, all smiles, and drew her in.

"So you did come—that's nice!" she said, with bewildering cordiality. "Kids, we won out after all! This is Linda," she said, thrusting her into the midst of a group

113

of boys and girls sprawled on the floor, draped over settees, and lounging in big chairs. "Introduce yourselves. . . . We're pretty informal here."

There was a general mumble, while Linda tried to remember such names as she could distinguish. One or two moved over to make a place for her and she could feel all their eyes on her, appraising or casual, interested or indifferent. There was a peculiar atmosphere in the room; she noticed it as soon as she entered, but she could not put her finger on what it was. It troubled her a little.

Some of the faces she recognized—Egbert Thorley and Clarence Fitts; Naomi Rysdale and Ginny Lothar. But aside from those and Helen, and one or two others whom she remembered seeing about the school, they were strangers to her. This was the group she belonged in, Helen said; they were her kind. They wanted her to be one of them.

Linda listened eagerly to their discussions, which they resumed, almost at once, where they had broken off when she came in. There were so many things, it seemed, that needed reforming . . . the talk ranged spasmodically from affairs in Washington to the restricted use of the swimming pool at school; from the muddleheaded foreign situation to the highhanded attitude of "certain people" who thought they could regulate school society and politics. Their voices rose; they interrupted one another. Naomi kept harping on her pet grievance—the fact that you had to park your bike according to number and not according to when you got there; and Egbert insisted on holding

114

forth, in long-winded fashion, on every subject that was offered.

"He's going to be a lawyer," Helen said, *sotto voce*. "Isn't he wonderful?"

Suddenly Clarence Fitts turned toward Linda. "You haven't said a word," he accused her. "Or don't you have any ideas?"

Linda said with spirit, "Of course I have ideas. But I wanted to hear first what your club was about."

"Well, spill one," he suggested.

She didn't like his tone, nor the implication—not very subtle—that she was without ideas.

"My main idea," she said, a little tartly, "is why don't you pick on some special thing you want reformed and then *do* something about it?"

"Hear, hear!" Egbert mocked. "Fools rush in where angels et cetera."

"What do you suggest we 'pick on,' as you elegantly put it?" Naomi inquired.

She wished she had never opened her mouth, but she felt goaded now to continue. "I don't care what it is. . . . I don't see how you can do much about Washington or Europe. But if you want to settle on some injustice at school, why don't you make a list and then *start?*"

"Such as—" someone in the back of the room asked belligerently.

"Well . . ." She floundered a little. "Well . . ." They had been talking about so many things it was hard to extract one from the multitude. "You mentioned some-

115

thing about the way the meetings are run—class meetings. Why don't some of you form a committee and the next time there's a class meeting get up, when the president asks for new business, and put in your motion for more representation, for more of a cross section of the Junior class?"

There was a stunned silence. Linda bore their stares with as much nonchalance as she could command.

"These things have to be threshed out first. . . . We have to have a plan of campaign. . . . There's no use jeopardizing our whole platform with an unconsidered movement . . ." That was Egbert, being pompous and cautious.

Clarence Fitts leaped to his feet. "Okay. Let's appoint Miss—uh, Marsh, a committee of one to state our grievances at the next meeting!" he brought out triumphantly, with a swift cutting glance at Linda.

There was laughter and applause.

"No, no," Linda protested. "I didn't mean—it ought to be—"

"You suggested the brilliant plan; you're the one to carry it through," he shot back, while the others nodded. "We'll present Miss Marsh with what we want said, and the way to say it, and she can do it."

They would not listen to her protests or accept her refusal. She had put her foot in it; it was impossible, it seemed, to withdraw without incurring their enmity.

"But *I* don't feel that way—so much," she said weakly.

116

"It's you who want things changed, who keep saying they must be changed. Why don't one of you—"

"You're appointed," Helen said crisply. "You're not a 'fraid-cat, are you? In the Reform Club we do whatever is asked of us, regardless of consequences. . . . We'll move on to other things now, and take up your duties at the next meeting."

Linda sat back, silenced but a little rebellious. She felt stimulated and at the same time oddly irritated . . . as if she had been in a fight whose outcome was left unsettled.

Helen took her aside after the meeting, made her wait until the others had gone.

"I'm proud of you, Lin," she said, with more warmth than Linda had ever heard in her voice. "You'll really make the grade. Don't let it fuss you. We're awfully outspoken here; and every person has to go through with what's put on him, no matter how he feels. That's the only way, of course." She put her arm around Linda's shoulders. "Did you give up the play?"

"Why—no," Linda said in surprise.

"But you were so early."

"I just got my part; I'm to learn it and report Wednesday," she explained. "Isn't it funny, too, how things happen? On the way out I met Everett Gore—"

"That drip!" Helen interrupted scathingly. "Burroughs' pet . . . and she can have him."

Linda ignored that. Privately she thought Everett Gore quite attractive. And how he could play!

117

"I don't know about that. . . . But he asked me to join the choir."

"Good grief! You didn't sign up with that bunch of yowling hyenas, I hope?"

"I can't sing," Linda said.

"And he knew it," Helen offered promptly. "That's why he asked. Puts him in a good light. . . . 'Come and join our big party; everybody welcome.' That sort of stuff. He takes good care to ask those he knows can't join. Gives him a 'rep' and saves the choir, at the same time, for his select bunch of cronies." Suddenly she gave Linda a piercing look. "You didn't tell him where you were going, did you?"

"Well—why, yes, I did."

"Did he ask?"

"He just asked, rather in fun, where I was going, and I told him." Helen bit her lip in annoyance and Linda said, "Shouldn't I have? Is this a secret organization?"

"Of course not, silly," she said sharply. "What did he say?"

Linda remembered, and gave a fairly good imitation. " 'Oh-oh,' he said. And then something about being sorry he'd held me up."

"You see?" Helen demanded. "That's what I mean. They're jealous of us. They don't want us to gain strength and new recruits. They don't want us endangering their little clique. We've got to keep mum about ourselves— who we are, and how many belong—until we're strong enough to act. Then watch 'em tumble!" she cried.

118

Linda felt uncomfortable. "You sound—you sound as if you'd get a kick out of it."

"That's what I'm working for; what we're all working for. And listen," she said with swift intenseness, "you're one of us now. They've accepted you; they gave you a job to do, and that means you belong. The dues are fifty cents; and one of the rules is that you've got to be present at every meeting, no matter what else turns up."

"I don't know that I can," Linda objected.

But Helen cut in, "You've got to. R. C. comes first with its members. Always. You have to sacrifice a *little* for something you believe in," she announced. "And don't go telling everybody you belong. We don't have to advertise; we pick our own members." She gave Linda a little shove. "That's orders, too."

CHAPTER SEVEN

"HEY, Lin!"

Linda wheeled, from her setting of the dining room table, at Bob's urgent voice.

"What now?"

He came in, frowning, hands in pockets. "What's for supper tonight?"

It was Mrs. Parsons' afternoon off, and Linda said proudly, "I made a shepherd's pie, and we have fresh green beans, applesauce, and peanut cookies. Hungry?"

"Oh, sure. But—but listen, Lin, aren't we going to have *any*thing out of a can? Gosh, what's the matter with us? Why can't we eat more out of cans?"

"Why, Bob Marsh, you ought to be glad I manage to feed you nearly all fresh food."

"Well, it's certainly hard on me. Here I am, yelling at everybody to bring in tin cans, and be sure and save all their tins and so forth, and they bring 'em in by the box. . . . But what do *I* have to show? Nothing, except maybe one a week." Linda laughed. He said belligerently, "It's nothing to laugh at. I'm captain, and I ought to set an example. But how can I, if we keep on eating fresh stuff all the time? Gosh, can't you plan to have some canned food once in a while? Our room's got to win the contest."

"You'll have to scout around the neighborhood, Bob. Have you canvassed everyone hereabouts? Get them to promise to let you have their tins. You can't expect the Marshes to furnish you with your full quota."

"I've been around," he said in a gloomy voice. "I've got everybody lined up I can think of. But it sure makes me look like a goon, ordering others around and not showing up with stuff from my own house."

Linda refused to be reproved. "You'll have to search harder over the town, then. It's not just tin cans, is it?"

"No, scrap metal—all kinds. I've gone over our cellar, and there isn't anything much I can use. We got rid of everything like that when we moved."

He sounded absolutely sunk at their lack of fore-thought.

Linda paused, in the act of straightening spoons and glasses. "I've a thought! Did you ever notice that old water tower on the edge of town—the one that they said belonged to the little factory that burned down?"

"Yep. So what?"

"Why don't you get that? You'd win the contest by a mile, and would probably get your picture in the paper besides."

Bob was staring at her. "You mean—"

"Of course I mean . . . go ahead and find out who owns it, ask if you can have it, get a scrap dealer to take

121

it down and pay for it—whoever owns it would get the money, of course—and let you turn it in as your class's contribution."

He was leaping around the table. "Jeepers, Lin, you've got a bean on your shoulders! Jeepers, why didn't *I* think of that?"

"It must be age, my lad." She grinned. "What do you think I go to high school for?" He was tearing out of the door. "Bob, not till after supper! No, absolutely not—it'll be ready in half an hour and you have to wash up first and clear out the pantry. You can go right afterward, or first thing in the morning."

"Aw, Lin—aw, Lin, for Pete's sake—"

"It'll keep," she advised. "*Two* people in this town aren't going to have a brainstorm like that on the same day. And, what's more, I'm not charging you a commission. Aren't you glad you have such a bright sister?"

He gave her a playful push. "Oh, you'll do. . . . If it weren't for Amy, I could be real happy in this house."

"What about me?" came from the doorway.

Amy, looking unusually tousled and grimy for her small, neat person, stood there holding an impatient and panting Jinks.

"Nothing about you," said Bob, going past in a hurry. " 'S just funny the way you manage to turn up for meals, when you're gone the rest of the time."

"Jinks wanted his supper. *I* wasn't hungry," she said with a quickness born of long years of this sort of thing.

122

"You look warm, and mussed, Amy. What have *you* been up to?" Linda wanted to know.

"Jinks got in a fight," she said with considerable pride. "He's just wonderful, Lin. Not only a watchdog, and bright as a dime, but a fighter, too. My, I certainly got a lot for fifty cents, didn't I?"

"Who—I mean what did he fight with?" Linda was anxious.

"Oh, just that awful old police dog down the block. He's been making faces at Jinks for weeks, but Jinks had lots of patience. Only today he must have *said* something, too, 'cause Jinks whipped around, quick as a wink, and nipped the dog in the leg and then they went at it. It *was* a fight!"

"Heavens!" Linda looked alarmed. "You aren't hurt, are you?"

"No, I tried to separate them; but I couldn't, and I wasn't worried 'cause I knew Jinks would win anyhow. But they knocked me down. . . . That is," she amended hastily, with a fond pat on Jinks' head, "the other dog did. Jinks never would, even when he was fighting."

"Well," said Linda, considerably relieved, "I'm glad you came off so well. Just a torn stocking, I see, and a black and blue elbow. You're pretty well suited with Jinks, aren't you?"

Amy's serious little face blossomed with a smile that transfigured it. "Oh, Linda, he's just—he's just—"

Words failed her, and she flung her thin arms around

123

Jinks' neck. Jinks choked a moment and then licked her face.

"Go and wash now, Amy. . . . And Jinks looks as if he could stand a brushing. Are you hungry?"

"Yes," Amy said, "but Jinks has to have his supper first. All the books say you shouldn't eat until you've fed your dog. . . . As if I would!" Linda heard her muttering indignantly as she led the willing dog kitchenward.

After supper Linda repaired to her room for a last going-over of her lines. She was letter-perfect in them, but that was no great feat; for she did not have many, and only a few odd pieces of business. She tried practicing gestures in front of her mirror, but it looked silly, somehow, and she went off into giggles. With her lines well in hand, she devoted all her time to trying out various voices. . . . "You still sound like western New York to me!" came, ghostlike, to her, disturbing her calm and making her self-conscious. Was that really true? Helen was outspoken. Was she, Linda, only fooling herself that she had made big strides forward toward her goal?

At rehearsal on Wednesday she was nervous and flustered, waiting in a kind of agonized suspense for what Miss Higham would say.

Miss Higham was harassed and disheveled. "If this shapes up before 1944 I'll be a surprised woman. . . . What's the *matter* with everyone? You must have your minds on something else." Then, with a flashing smile that took all the sting out of her words, "Not that I blame you. The world's much too exciting a place to put all your
124

efforts on a little play. But do try, please, to do me proud!"

They worked harder after that, but things went far from smoothly. Linda felt as if she'd been through the mill by five o'clock, when they were dismissed. Miss Higham had listened to her recital of her lines with an impassive face. Only once had her eye lit up at some unconscious bit of business on Linda's part.

"There—that's good! That was very good! Remember that, and use it," she said sharply, and Linda realized that she had actually forgotten herself, and her effect on the others, and had lost herself in the character she was portraying.

She didn't dare think too much about that character. She was taking the part of an old beggar woman. . . . Beggar women, in stories, always had whining voices. Was that why she had been chosen? Was there an insult behind this honor? Or was it, truly, because they were short a player?

The beggar woman wasn't the ordinary stock character, however. She was a woman who had seen tragedy in her life; she was supposed, the description said, to be dignified and pitiable, worn and beautiful. She was meant to represent the submerged forces of the world begging for a chance, for generosity and compassion and understanding. It was a pretty big assignment, if you looked at it that way. Would the audience ever fathom what she was supposed to put across? All the characters represented some quality other than their obvious one. Linda

125

wondered if the play, for all its apparent simplicity, wasn't too deep for the average perception of the average playgoer . . . particularly an audience of parents and classmates, prepared only to see their children or their friends taking a part on the stage. They weren't going to look for subtleties, for hidden meanings and poetic analogies. But it was a beautiful play. As it unfolded, as scene by scene took on shape and color and meaning under Miss Higham's inspired direction, Linda began to perceive how beautiful it was . . . how important even the comparatively small part of the beggar woman was in the whole, and she put all her heart into her portrayal.

It was important to have every bit of action, and of pantomime, just right. Miss Higham took her aside, worked tirelessly with her voice and intonation and the few restrained gestures she was to use. She marked white crosses on the stage floor to show Linda just where to kneel; where to cross over in front of Edith Merrick, the wealthy woman, at a given interval; how to place her body to form an effective shadow against the backdrop.

They rehearsed it again and again. Edith was splendid as the wealthy woman whose eyes had not yet been opened to charity and the forgiving heart. But Edith was temperamental—sometimes she played as if she were an actress born; and sometimes she was gauche and amateurish, as if she had never trod the boards before. Linda could see that Edith's excess of temperament was worrying Miss Higham. . . . How would she play on the night of nights? Sometimes she forgot where her station was to be, and other times she reached the spot as unerringly as a homing pigeon.

In spite of the tiring business of rehearsals, Linda was enjoying herself. For the first time since entering the school she was really working with a group, working for a unified effort and for a definite goal. She was on the stage so little of the time, however, that after the first two rehearsals, when she sat around and twiddled her thumbs, she decided to make use of her spare minutes and brought her knitting.

"Mercy, you work fast!" one of the girls said. "Where'd you learn?"

"My grandmother taught me," Linda said. "After I learned the stitches, we used to have races . . . and she often let me win. It certainly spurred me on!"

"The way you knit is the German method, isn't it?"

Linda said, "People call it that. But it isn't just German. It's used all over the Continent. And in England, too."

"Really?"

The other girl was polite, but a little unbelieving.

"Yes, I've seen pictures of the fishermen's wives sitting in their doorways knitting just this way. It's much faster than the other. And that's important nowadays, don't you think, with so much to be done?"

"I'd love to know how, but I always thought it was terribly difficult. . . . And German, you know. But if you say it's English, too—"

Linda smiled. "It is, really. And if you want to learn,

127

I'd be glad to teach you. See—it's simple. Like this. Hold the yarn over your left forefinger, just let it slide over . . . and pick it up with your other needle. . . . Watch."

Heads bent over, absorbed in teaching and learning, they got well acquainted. Linda felt a surge of pride; she was able to give something, to be of some service, however small. It gave her a sudden idea. It was such a startling one that she wondered for a moment whether she ought not to forget it. After all, who was she to start such a thing? How would it go over? What if she were rebuffed?

But then she thought, "I'd have to try; this is wartime. I've *got* to try and do something more than I'm doing. And this is something I could handle; I know I could, if they'd just let me."

She said, with a rush, "Martha, do many of the girls in your class—many of the girls you know—knit for the Red Cross?"

"I don't know. Why?"

"They're terribly in need of stuff, and I was wondering— Do you knit for them?"

"Oh, I did some squares, and a foot afghan; but it takes such *ages*—" She broke off. "Of course some of the girls are whizzes; they knit all the time. But not many, I guess." She wrinkled her brow, trying to think. "No, not more than a dozen that I can remember. I suppose they've all been so busy. There are a million things going on, you know. It's hard to find time to eat three squares a day, and as for dates—" She laughed.

"A million things to do," Linda said to herself soberly. "But not for me. And as for dates . . ." Resolutely she turned her mind away from that unprofitable channel, and returned to her idea.

"Would you knit for the Red Cross regularly, if others did? You know, if we had a kind of group or club . . . nothing stuffy, just sort of banded together to get a certain amount of work done?"

Martha Graham considered it. "Yes, I would. Why not? That is, I would if I didn't have anything too difficult to do. I'm not much at knitting, unless I get to be expert with this new German—I mean, Continental— way of yours; and that would take some time. But I'd do simple things, whatever they needed."

"That's grand!" Linda said happily. "You know what I'm going to do? I'm going to start forming a group right here among the girls in the cast. I'm going to ask every one of them—"

"Beggar woman! Beggar woman! Cue for beggar woman!"

Linda leaped like a startled fawn at Miss Higham's harassed voice.

"I'm sorry," she called breathlessly. "I was talking, and I—"

"We could all hear you talking," Miss Higham said a bit tartly. "Buzz, buzz, buzz. . . . I suppose it was important; but we do need concentration here, and if I have to follow up everybody for his entrances— Edith, take

129

that speech again—so Beggar Woman can come in promptly this time."

Linda felt somewhat dashed. There were a few snickers, which she tried to ignore; but in her haste to find her place she forgot her lines, and the scene had to be called again. She was thoroughly embarrassed by the time Miss Higham had had enough, and would have been glad to pick up her bag and go home. Yet something told her that if she didn't start now she never would. And this wasn't for herself, was it, she asked inwardly. This was for the Red Cross, for soldiers and civilians overseas, for sufferers from disaster in her own country.

She swallowed hard and went up to Edith.

"I'm planning a knitting group," she said. "Made up of girls who knit—right here in the school. For the Red Cross. And I hope you'll join. You can make whatever you please."

"I do anyhow," Edith said airily. "I don't have to belong to a group. Heavens, I've been knitting for them for ages. Have *you* just begun?"

But she had better luck with several others. It was a beginning, anyhow. Her plan was developing. Walking home, she enlarged and perfected it. The best thing to do would be to stop in at headquarters right now and talk it over with Mrs. Wing. Then she'd really be safe in going ahead.

Mrs. Wing listened attentively.

"I thought," Linda told her, "that I could line up the girls and get them to promise to do a certain number of

130

garments. I'd be responsible for getting the wool from headquarters, and seeing that the finished articles were turned in on time. I'd sew in the labels and block them, if necessary, and see that they passed specifications. And, first of all, I'd come here at regular intervals, have you tell me what you needed most, and then set the girls to working on those things—letting each one choose what she liked to make, as much as possible."

"I think it's a splendid scheme." Mrs. Wing was hearty with her approval. "That way we could give out a definite amount of work and know that it would be returned by a definite time. It would save a lot of wear and tear on us down here . . . there are so many things to look after. Perhaps you could get another group of girls, who didn't care about knitting, to come in and make bandages several afternoons a week—or even a few hours. It would all help tremendously."

It was arranged, then, that Linda would interview likely prospects. She would get the wool herself, distribute it; keep tabs on material and knitters; and return the finished garments, which would be listed, in all reports and publicity, as turned in by the Brookhaven High School Knitters.

"I'll bring my turtle-neck down tomorrow," Linda said happily, rising to go, "and get the first consignment of wool and the instructions."

"Good heavens, have you *finished* it?" Mrs. Wing was incredulous.

"Oh yes. I could do one a week, I'm sure," Linda said. "And thank you, Mrs. Wing, for letting me do this."

"Letting you?" Mrs. Wing repeated, with a pat on Linda's shoulder. "My dear, I can see that you're going to be a staff for me to lean on!"

Linda felt lighthearted and pleasantly purposeful. This was going to be fun . . . and she liked the thought of the responsibility. In her mind's eye she began to envision a staggering pile of knitted garments, all neatly folded and blocked, labeled "Brookhaven High School." And she would have been behind them. This was something with a meaning.

The staggering pile of blue and khaki and wine-colored garments suddenly melted away before the picture of a dream-dress in Kay's Dress Shop. Linda stopped short. It was just the sort of dress she had always wanted. There was a tight little bodice of lavender silk with velvet shoulder straps from which fell flower-edged ruffles over the upper arm. The girdle was a woven mass of the same tiny multicolored flowers, and they cascaded over the billowing pink skirt built of tier upon tier of sheerest net. She closed her eyes and saw herself rippling across the floor in that dress . . . the heavy rayon taffeta underslip rustling delightfully as she walked. She opened her eyes quickly, to be sure it was still there. And surely that price *couldn't* be right? "$19.50—reduced from $35.00," it said. It was the perfect dress; it was her ideal.

And it would be just the thing for the dance that was to follow the play. She hadn't let herself think too much about that dance. It could be heavenly . . . or it could be torture. She hadn't known what she should do about going. But now she knew. She *would* go . . . and in that dress. It would make all the difference.

A lot would depend on this dance. If she met boys, if they liked her . . . There would be the Junior Hop to look forward to in the spring. According to the girls' talk, Junior Hop was just about the most important date of the whole year. It made you—or broke you. If you were invited—and by the right person—it showed you rated; you'd arrived. But how could she dare to think of being asked to Junior Hop when she hadn't even been dated by a boy?

How marvelous that her allowance was still intact for the month! She could afford this easily. And she needed a formal, she told herself firmly as she swung open the door and passed into the empty, rose-carpeted salon of the Kay Dress Shop. If only it would fit, if only it would fit! she repeated under her breath in a kind of wordless prayer.

Miss Kay herself waited on her. "The dress was made for you," she sighed rapturously, standing back after she had slipped it over Linda's head. "But made for you! I knew it the moment you came in. It needs someone young and lovely . . ."

Linda held her breath, pulled in her stomach, and tried not to let it out as Miss Kay pulled and pushed and finally got the zipper closed down the back.

133

"It's rather tight," Linda said doubtfully. "I don't think I—I'm sure I couldn't breathe this way."

"But, my dear," Miss Kay said airily, "what is that? A mere trifle. See, I will fix it for you. Slit it here, run another row of flowers down the side—fortunately, I have some velvet just the right shade—and you'll never know the difference. Just a routine bit of alteration."

"Well," said Linda slowly. "Of course, with these saddle shoes—"

"Of course!" said Miss Kay at once. "One needs silver slippers, or satin ones dyed this lovely shade of lavender . . . or you could pick up any of the velvet colors. It would be too simply divine, as you girls say. Just close your eyes to the saddle shoes, my dear, and imagine your feet shod in silver slippers. Lovely!" she murmured, closing her own eyes and stepping back another pace. "It couldn't be better, really, if it had been made for you. With the exception of the bodice, of course, and that's so easily remedied."

Linda surveyed herself again and again in the long mirror. Oh, it was a dream of a dress. But—

"My arms look so long, don't you think? Of course I have long arms, but somehow they look like—like a gorilla's now."

"Gloves, my dear." Miss Kay solved that promptly. "You'll naturally be wearing long white gloves. It breaks the length beautifully. You have a pair?"

"No," said Linda. "I did have, but I don't think they'd fit any more."

134

"Here," said Miss Kay helpfully, rummaging in a drawer. "I have just the thing. Only one pair left. See what a beautiful kid they are—as soft as a baby's cheek. And such a lovely off-white."

"What size are they?" Linda asked, eying the gloves longingly.

"Six," said Miss Kay.

"But I wear size seven."

"Turn the hands in . . . roll them, you know. That's the smart thing to do. Dear, dear, one practically never wears the hands of the gloves with a formal! So what matter what size they are if the arms fit? And of course they will. Try them on."

So Linda tried them on, tucked in the hands, and looked at herself again. She stroked the soft kidskin, ran her hand lovingly over the crisp billowing net, touched the little flowers.

"So beautiful with your hair. Your hair is lovely!" Miss Kay twittered. "Like a cloud . . . A dark cloud over a garden of flowers. . . . My, that's almost poetry, isn't it? But I do love poetic effects."

Yes, her hair *was* nice, Linda thought. Thank Mary Clayborne for that. But, still, there was something . . . What was it?

Miss Kay read the doubt in her face. "When you've put on a touch of powder, my dear—just a dusting, you know, over that charming skin—and a touch, a mere *touch,* of color, for evening, for the lips . . . A dab of perfume, your slippers, a fur jacket, the long gloves . . . Oh,

135

can't you see it? Ah, to be young!" sighed Miss Kay with sentiment. "How I envy you young girls who can wear these lovely, lovely things! Shall I alter it, my dear, and send it up? Or will you stop in?"

"I'll stop in for it." Linda made up her mind suddenly. Perhaps Miss Kay was right. A bit of make-up, the proper accessories, would do wonders. At least she hoped so.

"Splendid! I'm so glad you're taking it. Now, just a little deposit . . . and then the alteration will be four dollars—quite a bit of work, you know; but I'll do it myself, and you will be *so* satisfied."

The dress. Alterations. Gloves. New hose. It was going to mount up. But Linda thrust out her chin resolutely. She was due for a special treat to herself. She had saved the money; she could afford it. And it was the kind of dress she had always wanted. If only she would look in it as she dreamed of looking!

With a new inner confidence—could it be because of the dress?—Linda methodically accosted a list of girls in her own and other classes. She got permission from Mr. Galbraith to give the group an official title incorporating the name of the school. Some of the girls promised immediately; some were doubtful, saying they would do what they could, but didn't dare promise; some were cool to the idea. They had so many other interests, they said.

"But it's for the Red Cross!" Linda would persist.

"Well," said one of them, "everything's for something . . . if you get what I mean. Glory, if you had to belong to everything people asked you to join! You've got to quit somewhere, and I'm quitting right here. I belong to so many things Mother says I'm a stranger at home."

"You could do it at home; you could do it anywhere," Linda said.

She was amazed at her own persistence, amazed at her brashness. But it wasn't for herself; it was for a cause, and one that she earnestly believed in. She had to make them see.

Sitting in on the next meeting of the Reform Club, she had her second idea. She had hesitated about going. She knew they were to draft the speech she was to make for them at the class meeting. But if she didn't go, they would think the worst of her. And she wanted people to like her; she wanted them to feel that she was willing to work for something she belonged to. It still seemed queer to her that they had picked on her for the job when there were doubtless a dozen others better qualified as to presence and ability. However, they were trying her out, she supposed, and Helen had said that they never gave a job to someone of whom they didn't approve. That made it all right, she thought. Yet a nagging little doubt and worry gnawed at her all during the meeting.

They took so *long* about everything! Why couldn't they state in clear, brisk terms what they wanted and believed was due them, and let it go at that? Why go over and over the same thing, turning phrases, being slyly ambiguous and unduly sarcastic? She was afraid the speech wouldn't go down; it would antagonize the hearers rather

137

than present their case. But they told her, a little rudely, that they knew what they wanted—hadn't they discussed it often enough?—and her job was to get up and give the talk, not criticize the way they were putting it.

She stood it as long as she could. Here were twenty idle people . . . idle, that is, except for their tongues, which kept up an incessant buzz.

In the first lull she said breathlessly, "Listen to me, reformers! You're wasting a lot of time here." They glared at her as one man, but she went on, "I don't mean with your talking—though I do think you could get a lot more done if you didn't talk a thing over so much. What I mean is: Here we all sit, doing nothing with our hands when we could be making bandages for the Red Cross. Mrs. Wing told me they were in need of every dressing they could turn out, and I know if we all fell to during our meetings we could do a marvelous amount of work. I'd be glad to collect the material each meeting and bring it out, and supervise—I mean I'd learn the foldings and teach whatever had to be taught, and I'd take the work back to headquarters. What do you say?"

Somehow she wasn't prepared for their answer. It burst upon her as a shock—a roar of disgruntled loud "No's!"

She looked from one to the other, unbelieving and surprised almost beyond speech.

"But why ever not?" she asked. "It doesn't take much concentration, and we could work for two hours—"

138

"Spare us the details," Clarence Fitts said. "You trying to be a reformer with a vengeance?"

"Why, no," she said. "I just thought—"

"Well, think about our problems then. One thing at a time. We need this club; we have a work to do. There's no use confusing ourselves and balling up the works by taking on something else. A house divided, you know . . ."

She said hotly, "But that's silly! What's divided about it? We've all got to do our bit in this war, and it seems to me the least we could do would be to turn idle time to some account, and surely this is a simple way to do it!"

"First thing you know Lady Marsh will be coming around with a doctor asking us to give our weekly pint of blood, I suppose."

"And to pay our yearly dues every seventh day."

"And knit sweaters and be airplane spotters during lunch hour."

"Let the waddly old ladies wear their veils down at headquarters. They've got plenty of time to make bandages. It's all they're good for—that and playing bridge. I'll bet they make all of ten bandages apiece an afternoon."

"Order!" said Clarence, with a smug look on his face. He had been enjoying her discomfiture along with the rest. "You see what happens—just *talking* about a divided interest. . . . Now let's get back to the business in hand. Egbert, you read that last paragraph again. I know we can make it stronger, put more of a punch in it."

139

So that was that. Linda was chagrined, and furious. She hadn't thought it of them. They were selfish and narrow-minded. They were unpatriotic.

She blazed at Helen. "They're a self-centered bunch! I'm surprised at them!"

"Keep it to yourself, then," Helen said, her mouth taking on that familiar thin line. "Seems to me it's a little early for you to begin criticizing. Just because they don't fall for a harebrained scheme that you cooked up right on the premises is no reason to call them names." Linda flinched. She *had* thought up the idea that very afternoon, right in their midst. But it was cruel to turn it back upon her that way. "You're hurt because your little idea wasn't swallowed hook, line, and sinker," Helen said shrewdly. "You've got to be bigger than that, Linda. You've got to put the common good above your own ambitions."

Linda said, with a rush, "That's what I *was* doing! The good of lots of people—the people the Red Cross works for—was coming before our own little selfish circle."

Helen gave her an unexpected pat. "Calm yourself. If you'll just keep all that fire for your speech at the meeting, you may do something yet for the common good."

CHAPTER EIGHT

THE formal hung on a padded hanger in her closet; beneath it stood her silver slippers; hose and gloves and slip, handkerchief and bracelet and compact, were on the bed. Linda lifted down the dress and smoothed its flounces lovingly. Then she got out her old suitcase, and laid in the other things. She would leave the dress till last, so that it would not muss. "Let's see"—she went over the list mentally . . . "comb, powder." She'd have to make a quick change in the girls' room after the play, so there was no use wearing her bunny jacket; her winter coat would have to serve. But no one would see her in it, anyhow. A feeling of excitement coursed through her veins. Tonight was the night. Might as well run through her part again before dinner.

She looked out of the window with an anxious frown. Bob was whistling noisily in his room, but Amy wasn't in yet. The early winter twilight had deepened into dark, and a heavy snow lay over the fences and lawns. She'd have to take a taxi both ways. Well, her father wouldn't mind. It was too bad he couldn't be here for the play, but he was called away more and more lately.

141

"It's a help to know you're in charge and so capable," he told her fondly. "I wouldn't rest easy these nights unless I knew that things would go on as well as if I were here."

Mrs. Parsons called that dinner was ready. They had set it forward tonight so that she would have plenty of time.

"Has Amy come in?" Linda asked, just to be sure.

"No, Miss Linda."

It wasn't like Amy to stay out after five. Could anything have happened? The excitement gave way to a mounting uneasiness.

"Gosh, I'm starved," Bob complained. "When do we eat?"

"Dinner'll spoil," Mrs. Parsons said tartly. "I could put a plate by for Miss Amy, and the rest of you ought to eat."

"We'll wait another fifteen minutes," Linda decided, gazing out of the window for a small form.

But when at six-fifteen she had not come, Linda crushed down her panic and began telephoning Amy's friends. No, she hadn't been there. . . . No, she hadn't been seen. . . . Yes, she'd walked home with Grace from school but hadn't stopped in. Said she had to take her dog for a walk.

"I'll go and rout her out, Sis," Bob promised. "After dinner. She's probably got her nose in a book down at the library."

Linda called the library, but no one answering Amy's

142

description was there. At six-forty-five she choked down her dinner, nervous and afraid.

"Do you think we ought to notify the police?" she beseeched Mrs. Parsons.

It was then that Amy came in. She dangled a broken leash from one small red hand, and her face was puffy and tear-stained. Her expression was tragic beyond words.

"Jinks," she croaked. "Jinks ran away." She held out the leash forlornly. "I've been looking for him all over town, and I can't find him. . . . Oh, Linda!"

"There, honey, come and eat something hot," Linda said. She rubbed the ice-cold hands and pulled off Amy's cap. "You're frozen, and you must be terribly hungry. Jinks will come back."

Amy's woebegone little face did not brighten. She held her fork in mid-air.

"But why *would* he run away, Lin? He had a good home, and nobody could love him more than me."

"He'll find that out," Linda soothed, and Bob said gruffly, "Cheer up, kid. Maybe he saw a rabbit or something. He'll be home pretty soon or, if he isn't, I'll find him for you. Gosh, it isn't such a big town!"

But nothing would console Amy. She would not eat, and the tears rolled silently down her cheeks.

"I think—I think I'd better stay home, Lin," she said finally, "in case he comes back. I'd want to be here, 'cause he would be cold and hungry. You don't mind, do you?"

143

"Of course not, honey. And you'd better drink some warm milk and curl up in bed."

"I won't sleep till Jinks comes home, though," she said defiantly.

"I could stay with her," Bob said. She knew he had wanted to see the play, and her heart swelled at this evidence of brotherly affection. "I could let him in, you know, in case Amy's asleep. . . . I mean, almost asleep," he amended hastily.

"That's nice of you, Bob," Linda said huskily. "I'll think of you both. And don't worry, honey. It will all come out right. Dogs get an adventuresome streak once in a while—you know, just as we do—and they want to see the world on their own. But they get tired of it pretty quickly and come back to the people who love them. Promise me you'll drink your milk and hop right in bed?"

Amy nodded; her eyes were red and her face felt hot.

Linda packed her bag hurriedly. This wasn't a very propitious way to start the evening, but she told herself that it would all come right. Amy would fall asleep; Bob would be here; Jinks would come home.

Just the same, Linda had a churned-up feeling in the pit of her stomach. It was the hurry and the worry, she told herself, added to the excitement of being in her first play. She had to acquit herself well—she had to!

The place was in a hubbub. Miss Higham was partly hoarse from last-minute directions. Stella Rivington had lost one of her shoes; Gladys Denny had developed a cold and was petrified that she would sneeze at the most dramatic moment in the play. The property woman had forgotten the pack of old newspapers, but one of the boys sprinted out to remedy that; and the electrician had put in a new blue bulb that gave a ghastly appearance to everything. Miss Higham was here, there, and everywhere at once. By five minutes to eight the atmosphere was torrid; but properties were in place, the light was repaired, the make-up was on all the characters . . . and the hall was beginning to fill up.

Linda, trailing her rags and running a bewildered hand over her wig of matted hair, managed to get a look through the small peephole in the curtain. The audience was in holiday mood and friendly; a continual hum of voices came welling up to the stage. It would have been so nice if someone out there had belonged to her . . . her father or Bob or Amy. But in a way she was glad circumstances had prevented it. She doubted if she could have been *more* nervous if they were here, but now at least she did not have to wonder how she was impressing them. She had only the audience to worry about.

Edith was hunched up on a packing case, where she was in everyone's way, mumbling her lines over and over, her eyes glazed and her hands twitching.

Miss Higham came up and scolded, "Put that script away this minute, Edith. This minute, do you hear? You know your lines as well as I do—this foolish cramming will only upset you. Stand up; relax; take ten deep breaths. . . . And *please* get off that packing case; somebody will break his ankle on you—or break yours, which would be just as bad!"

Edith muttered something under her breath and got up, reluctantly. Linda settled herself in the wings to watch . . . and at eight-twenty, only five minutes late, the curtain went up.

It was really a beautiful play. Linda was proud that she had been chosen to be in it. As the scene moved smoothly forward, she knew that the audience's real attention had been caught; there was scarcely a cough, and only an occasional chair squeaked. Though she had heard them a score of times and knew them all practically by heart, she listened to the lines now with new interest. Here was the completed play . . . not perfect, but moving; not too smooth, but still with its vitality intact—thanks to Miss Higham's indefatigable coaching. She had preserved the spirit of the play, at least. And this spirit was getting across.

The players were doing nobly, Linda thought; the prompter hadn't had to prompt once, and the light changes were carried out with quiet precision. Only Edith's acting, of them all, seemed a little spotty. Some of her speeches were given with great aplomb and distinction; in the very next scene she would stand woodenly, or stare out with slightly bulged eyes, as if forcing her reluctant mind to furnish her the words she was supposed to say. But she never entirely faltered; and Linda felt that perhaps she herself was being hypersensitive, that

146

she knew the play so well she fairly anticipated the lines.

When her own first cue came she entered confidently, dragging one foot a little as if she were lame, holding out her hands in a beseeching gesture. "Mind your voice," her inner self warned loudly. "Mind your voice; almost everything depends on that."

She moved forward across what seemed the vast stretch of stage to where Edith stood, haughtily awaiting her. Edith wasn't where she was supposed to be; she had moved at least six feet to the left. But Linda negotiated the distance without extra awkwardness or time lapse, and went into her speech. To her amazement, Edith, instead of standing still, walked away. Linda, in the spirit of her part, limped after her, imploring and anxious. After all, she thought quickly, that could happen, too . . . and, feeling thoroughly in character, she improvised her own movements accordingly.

Edith did the same thing, not once, but four times. Linda was first surprised, and then bewildered. She stilled the rising panic, and tried to see the scene objectively— so that she could give the best possible interpretation, the best possible pictorial effect. But it was difficult and confusing. Edith seemed to move with deliberate intent away from her, and twice she garbled her speeches so badly that Linda had to improvise hastily so that her own lines made sense.

At the climax, so carefully worked out for the place-ment of their bodies and the effect of the shadow on the backdrop, Edith was apparently unaware that anything

147

like that had ever been done, and Linda, in a kind of furious despair, was forced to make the best of an extremely awkward situation. Edith was so far upstage that, in order to get in front of her, Linda was uncomfortably close to the footlights; she could feel their heat against her crouching legs and back, and when Ellen stepped forward—which she should never have done—Linda said, between her teeth, "Don't! . . . I'm falling into the trough as it is!"

How much of it was evident to the audience Linda had no way of knowing. They didn't seem to think anything was wrong, for which she was tremulously grateful; and when the curtain went down, and rose again, the cast lined up to receive vociferous plaudits. Ushers came streaming down the aisles bearing sheaves of flowers. The cast bowed; the girls reached down happily for the tributes their friends and parents had sent. Linda was surprised . . . she hadn't known there were to be flowers. They had never done it at Wayneville. Her father would have sent her a bouquet, of course, if he had known. As it was—

Edith, standing beside her, wore a set smile and reached down for still another bouquet to add to her armload. A sheaf of roses was thrust into Linda's arms, too, and in the confusion and applause she bowed over the flowers, hugging them to her joyfully. Someone *had* sent her flowers, anyhow . . . someone *had* remembered her.

With the final bump of the curtain they trailed backstage. Edith came up to her, her face contorted and angry.

"How dare you—how *dare* you!" she cried, stamping her foot in a queer theatrical gesture.

Linda stopped, aghast. "Dare what?"

"Ruin my whole big scene! Crowding up in front of me, cutting me off from the audience! And balling up my lines! You did it on purpose, I know. Well, don't think you can get away with it! I was never so mortified and furious in my life!"

"You must be crazy," Linda said, her heart pounding. "I didn't do anything of the sort! It was the other way around!"

But Edith was trembling with rage; all at once her eyes widened and she let out a low shriek. "And this is the limit—the absolute limit! You low, mean . . . Give me my flowers!" She snatched the roses from Linda's arms. "There's my name on the card as plain as day. You're not content to steal my scene; you have to steal my flowers, too!"

Linda was utterly speechless. She felt as if she were in a bad dream.

"You can't say that to me—" she began, hurrying after Edith. "I won't stand for it. How did I know they were your flowers?"

"Your brother wants to see you, Linda." It was Ben Brixton, sticking his head around the dressing room door. "Sorry to interrupt. . . . Says he's got to see you right away."

Linda stopped short, as if an icy wind had struck her. Then her pulse raced in foreboding. "My brother? Where is he?"

"Out in the corridor. I told him to wait, you'd be right out. . . . Gosh, Linda, you were swell. I hardly recognized you, and you certainly put your All into that part. Congrats!"

It warmed her for a moment, that brief and coveted praise. And from Ben, who ought to know. For a second her hurt and dismay were miraculously soothed; then fear leaped forward again and shook her heart.

Bob was standing first on one foot and then on the other in an agony of impatience. His coat was wet, and his hair; and he was beating his mittened hands together.

"Bob! How long have you been here? What is it?"

"Just got here—five minutes or so, I guess. But it seemed like ages before you were all done bowing. . . . Lin"—his young face worked with his effort to control it—"Lin, you'd better come home right away. It's Amy. She's sick."

Linda took Bob by the shoulder. "What's the matter? Have you called the doctor?"

Bob nodded. "I went to Mrs. Clayborne—I didn't know which one to telephone—and she called hers. He's there now. They said I better get you as soon as I could; and we couldn't telephone the high school, of course, so I came over and waited. . . . Oh, Lin, she's got the most terrible chill! She just shakes the bed. It's pneumonia, the doctor says. And now she's got fever, and she keeps calling for Jinks, Jinks, all the time. I couldn't stand it; I was glad to have a chance to come out."

"Is Mrs. Parsons with her?"

"Yep, and Mrs. Clayborne. They're doing all they can; only they can't do anything."

Linda gasped. "You don't mean—"

He looked up into her shocked face. "No, no. I mean the doctor says you give 'em these sulfa drugs and then you wait. But she breathes so queer, and she keeps tossing around and calling Jinks."

Linda said firmly, "Find Ben Brixton, Bob. Ask him to let you into the principal's office, where there's a phone. The office is locked now. Call a taxi. Tell him to hurry. I'll get my suitcase and wraps, and meet you at the front door."

He sped off, and Linda, her hands scarcely knowing what they did, jumbled her clothes—the underthings and slippers, the lovely dress she had packed with such high hopes—back into the suitcase helter-skelter. She put on her galoshes, flung her coat over her rags, wrapped a scarf over her matted wig.

Miss Higham said, "Where are you going, Linda? Surely you're staying for the dance?" Linda told her hurriedly, and Miss Higham said with warmth, "Oh, my dear, I'm so sorry! I shall pray for good news. These sulfa drugs do wonders, you know, when it's caught in time, and I'm sure this was."

"I—I hope so." Linda's lips quivered.

"Keep your heart up. That helps a patient, too. . . .

151

And I must tell you, Linda, that you were splendid. I'm proud of the way you handled a very difficult situation. Don't think I didn't realize it. You did beautifully."

Bob reported that the taxis were all out; they could send one later, but he had said not to bother.

"We can walk it," he said. "I'll carry the bag."

They plodded through the deep snow of the silent streets, not talking, panting a little with their hurry. A hundred pictures went through Linda's mind: Amy as a baby, Amy with her first haircut, Amy making mud pies . . . Amy and Jinks. It was that which was unbearable.

She threw off her wraps and raced upstairs. There was a bright light on, and the doctor, looking grave, stood beside the bed. Mrs. Clayborne sat near the window, and Mrs. Parsons stood in the far doorway.

Linda went closer. The restless little figure stirred and tossed. Her eyes widened.

"Go away!" she cried hoarsely. "Go away!" pointing at Linda. "You're a witch, and you stole my dog. Go away—I hate you!"

With a shock Linda realized how she must look— bedraggled, with matted hair and dark make-up.

"She's delirious," the doctor said. "She doesn't know you. She'll be better soon. But it might be well to change."

Linda knew it was foolish, but she was close to tears. She bathed her face, combed her hair, put on soft slippers and a warm dress. No nurse was available, the doctor said, but Linda and Mrs. Parsons felt they could manage

152

between them. And Mary Clayborne volunteered her services wherever needed.

It was a hushed household for the next few days. Mrs. Parsons proved a tower of strength; her salty common sense and matter-of-fact manner were a great help toward stabilizing Linda's emotions. Bob said he had an errand the following morning, and she did not question him. It was touching to see him tiptoeing about with elaborate caution, to hear him ask a dozen times if there was something he could do. Linda and Mrs. Parsons devised a schedule of bedside watching and household care that they felt would work out, and Mrs. Clayborne came in with an ice bag and orangeade, with chicken broth and custard.

Amy slept most of the day. Her fever had gone down; she was more rational. But she kept tossing from side to side, and even in her sleep tears rolled down her cheeks. The name of Jinks was on her tongue, waking or sleeping.

"Has he come home yet, Lin? Don't forget to give him something to eat right away. . . . And look at his paws, Lin; maybe he's got ice between his toes and it hurts."

Up and downstairs . . . up and down. Telephone, doorbell, cooking. Linda was tired by late afternoon; she went out on the porch and rescued the evening paper, sodden in a snow pile, and held it before the fire to dry it out. She'd cast an eye over the headlines before she went up again. How far away world events seemed! How immaterial now were Guadalcanal and Buna, Tunis and

Stalingrad . . . sugar rationing and fuel shortage. The world revolved around the figure upstairs; everything in her little world depended on whether Amy got well.

Suddenly her eyes widened, fastened with unbelief on a bold two-column caption: "Brother Begs News of Lost Dog for Sick Sister." There was a subheading, too: "Champion Salvage Captain of Morrison School Begins Hunt for Pup; Asks City-Wide Help." It could only be Bob. It *was* Bob. She read on, fascinated and thrilled. They had done a good story. It would have set anyone to combing the area for a "small wire-haired fox terrier (almost), with frisky manner, brown saddle, black nose, intelligent eyes, capable of many tricks, and the adored companion of a little girl tossing in delirium and calling out for Jinks. See page 8."

Linda turned obediently to page eight. There was Bob's picture—a sober Bob, hair slightly on end as it always was when he had snatched off his cap. Underneath was a boxed write-up about Bob's achievement in bringing in the highest score of any captain in the Brookhaven schools. How he had salvaged the forsaken water tower, gotten Mr. Iraquadi to buy it at his best rates and dismantle it. How he had stood over him while he weighed it and wrote out the total, and then in triumph turned in the figure which had put Bob's class so far ahead of the others that no one else could approach it.

"It wasn't just me," the *Courier* quoted Bob as saying. "My sister—my other sister, Linda; she's in high school

154

—thought it up because I wanted metal and we don't eat enough out of cans. I've got two swell sisters. But it's about Amy I've come. If you can put a piece in the paper about how she isn't going to get well till Jinks is found, somebody ought to turn up who's seen him; and if they'll tell me, I'll go and get him. I've got to find Jinks, because if I don't Amy won't ever get over it."

There was his telephone number, and his address; any calls to the *Courier* by sleuths who had found, or thought they'd found, Jinks would be promptly relayed to the waiting Bob Marsh.

Linda smiled tenderly, reading the account. That was where Bob must have gone this morning. He had a head on his shoulders, that youngster. And an overwhelming love for his sister. She heard him, just then, coming in the front door, closing it with unwonted care.

"Bob," she called unsteadily, "Bob, come here! Jinks is all written up and your picture's in the paper!"

Bob looked at it sheepishly.

"I wanted them to put it in about Jinks," he said. "But gosh, I didn't think they'd tell about me. They kept asking questions, and then they asked if I minded if one of the men took my picture; but I never thought they'd put me in, too. . . . Lin, do you think it'll help find Jinks? . . . How is she, Lin?"

"Better, dear. A little. She slept nearly all afternoon. You can take her supper up, if you like."

But Bob shook his head. "I'll carry the tray up for

155

you," he said. "Only I don't want to go in and stay. If I do she'll ask me about Jinks, and I won't know what to say."

For the next few days—since school had begun the long holiday—Bob gave up all his usual activities. He did not go sledding or skating; he did not even go near his chemistry shed. He spent most of his time within leaping distance of the telephone. Linda could hear him, a dozen times a day: "Yep, this is Bob Marsh. . . . You did? Where? . . . Well, thanks; I'll go and see. . . . I sure hope so."

But all his spurts of investigation, following the telephoned clues, were fruitless. After each one he came home more dejected, and more determined, than ever. Linda's heart was torn between his despair and Amy's urgent pleading for news of her beloved Jinks.

It was a queer holiday season. Not at all the way she had fondly planned it weeks ago. Then she had imagined them all together . . . excursions to town and possibly to New York with shopping lists. Wrapping packages. Choosing a tree. Making special cookies, and a big mince pie for her father. The excited whispers and air of mystery that the Christmas season always brought; and something deeper this year, something beyond the personal.

Now the cherished little home plans were shelved; shopping was forgotten, the tree only a possibility if, and when, Amy got well. There would be no dinner with them all together . . . Amy would still be a convalescent

156

upstairs on a restricted diet. There would be no special treats, because it wouldn't seem fair when Amy couldn't share them.

On the doctor's advice she did not telegraph her father to come home. It was a grave decision, but he assured her that it would not be necessary—not if everything followed the proper course, as he felt confident it would. It was comforting to lean on his authority. She knew how busy her father was, how difficult it would be for him to get back, and how any news of Amy's illness would disturb him. So, a little hesitantly, she wrote, "Amy has a bad cold, but we're keeping her in bed and taking good care of her." The doctor promised that at the first turn for the worse he would let her know so that she could reach her father.

The sulfa drug worked wonders . . . physically. Amy improved almost at once. The fever died down; the congestion was conquered. It became chiefly a matter of convalescence, the long pull upward. But Linda knew, watching the sober little face and the big eyes, that only Jinks' return could make Amy truly well.

When Amy sat up, for her first afternoon, with Mrs. Parsons standing guard, Linda felt it was safe to slip away for a little and see about her knitting group. She had various collections to make . . . and if she had the garments all together she would be able to inspect and block them, and she could sew in the labels while she sat with Amy.

She breathed deep of the frosty clear air. It was only

157

a week since that dreadful night of the play, but it seemed to Linda that years had rolled over her head. It was good to be out in the wintry, glittering afternoon. In spite of herself, her spirits lifted. The shops were gay with traditional decorations. She stopped and bought some holly and a tiny potted tree for Amy's room. They would have their celebration there. She bought Amy a woolen scarf and mitten set, Bob an alligator belt, Mrs. Parsons a box of stationery. It was fun to shop again. Twice she was waited on by high school students whom she recognized.

"Lots of us are doing this," one of them told her. "Bill Fellowes is a floorwalker in a shoe store. The shopkeepers say we aren't half bad, either!"

Everybody was busy, doing his share—doing something for the war effort, or to help in the community. Linda felt as if only she were lost in the backwater . . . anxious to swim with the others but unable to catch up with them.

When she called at Jane Griggs' home for the promised sweater, Mrs. Griggs said she didn't know anything about it. Jane certainly never knitted on a sweater that *she* knew about, and so of course she couldn't say anything about it. She was inclined to close the door on Linda— for which Linda could scarcely blame her, since it was bitingly cold. But neither did she ask Linda in.

"You see, Mrs. Griggs," Linda hurried to explain while the door inched shut, "Jane promised to have it done by this Friday. I said I'd call for it. I have to turn in my quota each week, and Jane—"

"Well, you'll have to see her about it," Mrs. Griggs said shortly. "I'm busy now . . . and I'm sure Jane won't have any time to do anything, either. She's very popular, Jane is. Out every day, and most evenings as well."

"But she *did* do it, Mrs. Griggs," Linda tried to say. "I'm just here to get it. Will you ask her to let me know—"

"Call her up sometime." The door was definitely closing now. "I think it's foolish to knit while there are so many things for girls to do. They're only young once. I think you must have Jane mixed up with somebody else."

Linda felt annoyed, but not really disturbed. Perhaps Jane knitted only at school or at her friends' homes, and her mother didn't know about it. She had no faintest idea that she would have any difficulty straightening the matter out once she got in touch with Jane.

The trouble was that she couldn't get in touch with Jane. When she telephoned, Jane was out or unable to come to the phone; or Mrs. Griggs was too busy to go and ask her.

"Anyhow," Mrs. Griggs said at last, with meaning emphasis, "if she's done with it you'll hear from her. There's no use calling up about it all the time. I'm awfully busy these days."

Linda turned away from the telephone with a baffled feeling. Still, she tried to rationalize, she supposed there would always be some difficulties of this kind, some little misunderstanding or annoying delays when you were working with a number of people who did not necessarily feel bound by any rules because it was entirely volunteer work. She'd iron it out soon. A sharp ringing of the telephone before she had crossed the room brought her up short.

Maybe that was Jane now. Perhaps it was another call from someone who thought he'd seen Jinks. Or the *Courier* . . . a man from the *Courier* called daily. "Have you found Jinks yet? Be sure and let us know. We want to run the follow-up story."

But it proved to be Carol. "How's your sister, Linda? . . . A little better? Oh, I'm so glad. Because then I hope you'll be able to come to my party Monday night."

Linda had trouble in controlling her voice. A bid from Carol Burroughs! At last . . . a bid to her house, to a party! Monday was just two nights away. . . . But Amy would be well enough to leave. And she had her new formal, which she hadn't even had a chance to wear. What could be a more festive occasion?

Carol was saying, "I know it's short notice, but it's my birthday and we were going in to New York to celebrate, but I thought it would be much more fun to have a party out here. Come at eight-thirty . . . we're going to dance."

Linda said huskily, "I'd love to come, Carol. Thanks for thinking of me."

"Grand! See you Monday, then."

CHAPTER NINE

SHE wanted to shout it out, to run and tell somebody. She'd been invited at last into the circle, Carol's circle, the place where she longed to be. Not just spoken to at school, but asked to her home. Not just for an afternoon, but for a formal party. It was silly to be so excited, she told herself sternly. Just the same, the excitement would not be downed; it mounted from hour to hour.

She had always wanted to see Carol's home. Hadn't she heard enough about it at school? Casual remarks dropped by those in the know, innuendoes and wonderings by those who had never been inside. Hadn't Helen told her that Mrs. Burroughs was known for the parties she gave for Carol, and everybody was dying to be invited? Helen had been scornful of the gaga way some of the girls had acted about it . . . as if it were a bid by royalty and all that. *She* didn't see it that way, she intimated. But what Helen had said, and the way she had said it, had only whetted Linda's interest further.

Helen . . . All at once Linda put her hand to her cheek. Helen and the Reform Club. The Reform Club meeting was Monday night.

161

She couldn't go, of course. She didn't really want to go. If it came to choosing between a meeting of the club and a party at Carol's, who could expect her to choose the club? She'd call Helen and explain it right away. Of course Helen had been quite stern about impressing on her that a member was supposed to attend all meetings, but naturally there'd be an out occasionally. And this was an occasion.

She was totally unprepared for the venom of Helen's reply. "Why, you little backslider, you! All La Burroughs has to do is crook a finger at you and you run. You drop everything. Even a solemn date. You know I told you it was obligatory to come to meetings."

"I might have been sick," Linda said.

Helen snorted. "You know what I mean. You *aren't* sick . . . and you're supposed to come. It's a very important meeting. You've got to be there."

"But I can't, Helen," Linda said patiently. "That's what I'm trying to tell you. I accepted Carol's invitation without remembering that Monday night was the club's meeting. It's no wonder I forgot—we've always met in the afternoon, and it was just the other day you told me you'd changed it to the evening."

"So that's all the importance you attach to it. You forgot!" she mimicked unpleasantly, even to the intonation of Linda's voice.

Linda said stiffly, "You don't have to believe me. But it's true."

"You can tell Carol you had a previous engagement."
162

"Oh, I couldn't!" Linda was appalled.

"It's done all the time. You mean you don't want to. I see through you—don't think you aren't pretty transparent when it comes to wanting to be in with Carol and her smart gang. If that's all we mean to you, we and what we stand for—"

Suddenly Linda lost patience. It seemed to her that Helen was making a mountain out of a molehill, was deliberately provoking her.

"Oh, don't be a goon," she said sharply. "You're just picking a quarrel, and I won't quarrel. I can't come this time, but I'll be there next. You can tell me what happened."

"I certainly won't. And if you don't come this time, you're out. For good and all. I'll see that you're dropped like a hot potato."

By sheer will power Linda hung on to the shreds of her temper. "Gosh, you make it sound like a real threat!"

"It won't stop there, either," Helen said darkly. And that *did* sound like a threat. "We invited you in only because I felt sure you would make a member. If you're going to drop out every time you get what you think is a more interesting date, you don't belong to us and we don't want to have anything to do with you."

Linda said, with as much nonchalance as she could muster, "Done lecturing, teacher?"

"Yes," Helen returned with tartness. "And when they drop you, don't come crawling back to us begging to be taken up again. Because you won't be. I'm ringing off

163

now. But I just want you to think about one question. Maybe you won't feel so flattered when you dope out the answer. Why did Carol invite you over the phone at the last minute, when she sent everybody else a written invitation a week ago? Think *that* over, sap."

There was a click at the other end; and Linda sat staring at the telephone, amazed beyond action. A voice said patiently, "Number, please? . . . Number, please?" before she was aware that she still held the instrument in her hand.

She replaced it and got up angrily. Well, that was that! Over and done with! She was no longer a member of the Reform Club. It was too bad she hadn't resigned before she was kicked out. It made her furious to think Helen had been able to do that to her. But, in another queer way, she was glad it was done. She hadn't thought much about it before; yet the feeling had always been there, underneath. An uncomfortable feeling. She had never really enjoyed the meetings; she had squirmed a little over their incessant wrangling and dissatisfaction, their crabbing and picayune "reform" spirit. She hadn't wanted to be "one of them." Not after she found out what they were. But it would have been hard to get out. Now they had solved it for her. They didn't want her any more.

She wondered, with a swift stab of pleasure, whom they'd get now to do their pleading for them at the next class meeting. She saw with sudden clarity that they had picked her because she was new, because she wasn't yet on to them, and because they felt she would be flattered by having an important job to do. She was well rid of them.

But that last jibe of Helen's rankled. She tried to put it out of her mind, and couldn't. It bobbed up at unexpected moments, demanding to be faced. Why *had* Carol invited her at the last minute? It was true, too, that Carol had written the others some time ago . . . she remembered now hearing several girls exclaiming over their invitations, talking about what they'd wear. It hadn't sunk in then; now she remembered it with uncomfortable vividness.

In other words, she hadn't been included in the original scheme. Someone must have dropped out, and—perhaps after trying everyone else—Carol had decided to ask Linda Marsh, just to keep the couples even. Not because she wanted her, but because she had to have somebody and Linda was a last hope.

It took all the joy out of it. Of course Carol *had* said she wanted her, was delighted she could come. But that was the sort of thing a hostess *would* say, no matter what she thought. And Helen had said . . . But Carol had said . . . She went around and around till her head buzzed, and all she knew was that she was acutely unhappy. The party she had looked forward to with pleasure and excitement became, as the hour neared, an ordeal to go through. She toyed with the idea of not going at all. That way she would be spared any humiliation. But she couldn't quite bring herself to that. . . . Maybe Helen was right, and she was like all the rest. She'd do anything to get to the Burroughs', to be considered one of Carol's set.

She dressed slowly, with reluctant fingers. She brushed her hair desultorily, and fumbled with her slippers.

"Let me see you!" Amy called impatiently.

Linda went and stood before her small critic.

Amy said at last, "It's—it's a pretty dress, Lin."

Linda's heart sank. "Don't you like me in it?" she forced herself to ask.

"Of course I like you . . . in anything," Amy said with a queer grown-up air. "You're pretty. And the dress is pretty. I don't know, you don't just seem—"

"We don't go together,' I suppose," Linda said, more sharply than she knew. "Is that it?"

Amy's little face flushed, but she said stoutly, "I guess so. I like your blue crepe better."

"That's just an afternoon dress. Everybody's wearing a formal. I thought it was a *lovely* formal." Linda started out firmly, and then she wavered. "I did think so. But now, when I see myself in it, it isn't what I thought it was, either. Or perhaps it's myself. The clothes I like in the window never seem to look right on me when I get them home. I *hate* having such big bones, and being so tall. Nothing ever looks right. It's horrid!"

Amy's gaze had returned to the window. She peered anxiously at the small patch of snow lit by a street light. "If you see Jinks, Lin—or anybody says they've seen him—"

Linda swooped down with a swift rush of tenderness.

166

"Yes, darling. Please go to sleep now. I *know* Jinks will come home soon." . . . "If he doesn't," she thought bleakly, "Amy will never be the same; Amy will never get well."

As the taxi wound up the Burroughs' drive, between snow-covered evergreens, Linda knew a moment of utter panic. How would she face it? Who was going to be there? Why hadn't Carol given her some idea? What if she had to meet Edith face to face? . . . And it was going to be awkward, arriving alone this way. Was she late or early? She couldn't be sure. If only Carol had arranged to have one of the boys call for her! But perhaps none of the boys wanted to call for her. In her mind she could hear them protesting, "Her? Gosh, why pick on me?"

She felt cold and stiff with trepidation when the maid opened the door. Her confused eyes had a blurred impression of vistas of bare polished floor, walls and lights looped with Christmas decorations, and a big curving stairway. There was talking and laughter from the rooms to one side of the wide hall.

Then Carol came rushing through. "Why, Linda! I'm so glad you're here. Are you frozen? . . . Just go upstairs and leave your things, Lin. The room on the left; a maid's there. And hurry down!"

Carol looked lovely, Linda thought with a flash of appreciation—very lovely in a thick gold silk that brought out her long slim lines and coppery hair. It was very simple . . . it must be the cut that made it so effective. Or else Carol was one of those lucky people who could wear

167

anything. Her only ornament was a string of olivines in a dull filigree setting.

The rooms opening off the upper hall offered tantalizing glimpses of color—soft pastel-toned rugs and subdued chintzes and gay upholstered chairs. Linda would have liked to linger in each one. Which was Carol's, she wondered. How would Carol have done her room?

The maid took her wrap and fur-topped galoshes. Linda ran a comb through her hair and touched her face with powder; she twisted in front of the mirror and needlessly adjusted the tiers of her *bouffant* skirt and toyed with the velvet flowers. But finally there was nothing more to be done; she would have to go down.

She hesitated on the lower landing, and Carol saw her and detached herself from a group she was talking to.

"Come and meet Mother and Dad."

Mr. Burroughs was tall and gray-haired, with a young face; Carol was strikingly like him in build.

And Mrs. Burroughs, petite, blonde, and animated, said, with a warm pressure of her hand, "I'm so glad to know Carol's friends. Carol has told me what a help you were to her when I was gone. You must be quite a housekeeper, my dear!"

Linda flushed with pleasure, happy that Carol had given credit where credit was due, and pleased that Mrs. Burroughs had mentioned it to make her feel at ease.

"I had to learn," she said now, "when Mother was ill; and after she died I had to take charge of the house, and of my brother and sister too."

168

Mrs. Burroughs said, with genuine interest, "Carol was very much impressed. I think it does every girl good to know what it means to manage a household, but to learn so young—and to be so successful—is quite remarkable. You learned the hard way!"

"Don't get started on recipes, for heaven's sake," Carol laughed, "or Mother will keep you here all evening. She thinks your cranberry tarts are a prize, and she's been after me to get some more gems from you whenever I can; only I always forget. . . . Come over here, Lin—you'll excuse us, won't you, Mother?—some more of the gang have just arrived."

Ben Brixton was there, his flaming crest towering over the others, and Jimmy Post; Dana Goodwin and Lillian Travis; Gene Trumbull, Loring White, and Joan Daniels; and a dozen others whom she knew by sight but had never really spoken to.

Carol thrust her into their midst with an airy "You know everybody, I think, Lin; and if you don't, speak to them anyhow," and was off to greet her new arrivals.

They tossed her careless greetings and resumed their conversations. Linda listened, in mounting bewilderment; half a dozen of them were going on at once.

"Jiggsy Martin said the screwiest thing yesterday! Wait till you hear! You know he's working at Callender's, and Bibbs met him on the corner—"

"If we have to do that again, I'm through! Really, I never put in a worse hour in my life. You should have

169

seen me when I got home. I looked as if I'd been to the wars, and Mother demanded—"

"How should I know? I've been up to my ears. Laura said she'd let me know by Monday sure, but I haven't heard a peep out of her. And what are we going to do if she reneges?"

"Did you hear that? Listen, everybody, Jimmy made a joke! It's screaming—"

"I didn't mean—"

"You said—"

"What did he do it for, then? We'll have to be careful. With all those committees shaping up, you'd think someone would have a thought—"

The words bubbled and flowed around her, leaving her, high and dry, on an isolated island. She was in the midst of them, but not part of them.

Now and then she caught a familiar name, or a phrase which gave her the meaning of the whole; but for the most part it was Greek to her. Meaningless sounds. Incidents to which she was a stranger. A life at school that must have been going on while she was there, but that she knew nothing about. They didn't mean to be cruel, she knew; but they all had the same interests and they were so closely knit that the most ridiculous jumble of words meant something to them. She wanted to break away—they probably wouldn't even know she had gone— but she could not move from the spot where she stood. She wished intensely that she was back with Mrs. Burroughs, talking safely about recipes and her family. She looked for Mrs. Burroughs' small well-coifed head, and did not see it. She would have to stay here, then, till she was rescued, or they talked of something she could take part in.

To ease some of her embarrassment Linda studied the room. Rugs had been taken up, and furniture pushed back against the wall; but she could form a good picture. A fire burned on the wide hearth; French doors led to an inviting solarium with deep chairs and troughs of flowers; over the mantel was a striking portrait of Mrs. Burroughs. Linda's appreciative eyes picked out pieces of brass and copper, books in soft leather bindings, a Chinese table of gold lacquer, and an odd cabinet of old silver in the library beyond. There were flowers everywhere; massed greens, low bowls of roses, a long basket of carnations spicing the room. On either side of the fireplace two tall standards bore seven lighted candles, their flames wavering brightly in the scented gusts of air.

"Well," came a welcome voice at her side, "if it isn't one of our reformers!"

She looked up to find Everett Gore there. And Carol holding him by the arm proudly. Everett was Carol's special friend.

As if by magic everyone stopped talking. Now there was silence; now attention was focused on her, when she would have given anything to have them ignore her.

The crowd was looking from Linda to Everett, for some sort of explanation. Words, desperately needed words, stuck in Linda's throat.

Everett said, with a quizzical glance at her, "I didn't know she belonged, either, till she threw me over about the choir for a meeting of the reformers. . . . And, by the way, didn't I hear they were having a meeting tonight? How come?"

He meant, of course, how did it happen that she was here. She forced her stiff lips to say, "I don't belong any more." . . . "Please, please," she prayed silently, "don't let him ask me why."

"No? Well, that's good. One girl saved for society, anyhow. I hope you don't mind my saying so, but they're sort of a crazy bunch. Don't you think?"

She could only nod, grateful that he had put into words what she had been thinking recently. Grateful, too, that he had squared her somewhat with the crowd.

"Too bad," he said, "that no one told you about 'em before you got in with 'em. You being new here . . . What do they want to reform, anyhow?" he asked conversationally.

"You," she said. Everybody burst into laughter, and she was startled. "I mean—I mean people like you."

She waved her hand at Everett Gore and then on to include all of them.

"But why?" someone demanded. "I'll admit we aren't perfect. But how do we need reforming?"

"Oh, why go into it? I'm afraid I'll hear something," another voice said banteringly. "Come on, perfectly swell dance music going to waste. Who'll step on my toes?"

172

And the discussion broke off before it started. Linda drew a quivering breath.

She felt that she had been spared some sort of ordeal, but that it was not over yet. Thoughts raced through her head, half-formulated decisions and something else, besides, that she couldn't quite catalogue. Later, perhaps. Now her whole attention was focused on whether or not she would be asked to dance, too, or left standing alone. There was an awful moment of panic . . . and then, like a good hostess, Carol brought up Sam Hellburn, a new arrival.

"Linda's been waiting for you . . . and you came late so you could dance with Linda, I know," she laughed.

And Linda found herself skimming and swooping over the floor in the strong grasp of the class treasurer.

She danced well, even though she was almost as tall as he. He told her so, frankly; and his approval must have spread to the other boys, for after that she had no lack of partners. The evening winged by in a rosy haze of music, the scent of flowers, the delightful sound of laughter and banter in which she had a part. It wasn't so hard to talk to individuals, in spite of not knowing them well, she discovered, once she felt that she was being accepted. It was being thrust into a group where you did not know what they were talking about that made it difficult. Her cheeks flushed with the exercise and the stimulant of happy moments; she felt lighthearted and as if her feet had wings. Her eyes sparkled; her hair

173

floated around her shoulders, covering the multicolored velvet flowers; her wide-tiered skirt billowed and swayed about her.

"I'm parched!" she gasped at last, after a particularly violent conga, and leaned, laughing and gasping, against the mantel.

"Punch is in order," Buzz Dean said promptly. "Any special kind—if I have a choice?"

"Pink," she laughed, "with a touch of green and lavender to match my dress."

"Okay," he said. "With some blue strawberries in it, I suppose. And would you like it wet?"

"Oh, very. . . . Just hurry. Anything will do in a pinch."

"Any punch in a pinch," he muttered, and then, liking the sound, "Any punch in a pinch! Say, that might do for a class motto."

"It sounds like a prize fighter's slogan, if anything," she told him, and watched him battling his way across the room and through the crowd around the punch table.

When he came back he carried two glasses, brimming full.

"One for you, *and* one for you," he said, presenting the first with something of a flourish.

Someone pushed him from behind; and the liquid spurted in a devastating trickle down the bodice of Linda's dress, over the girdle, and down the tiered skirt. She watched the widening purple stain with a kind of fascinated horror.

"Oh, I'm sorry! I'm darn sorry!" Buzz muttered, in
174

miserable confusion. He set the glasses down on the mantelshelf and whipped out his handkerchief. "I'll slaughter that ox who shoved me."

Carol came up then. "What happened? . . . Oh, Linda, your dress! How awful!"

"It—it was *wet* punch all right," Linda managed.

"You're a sport," Buzz said, with wan gratefulness. "But gosh, I can't tell you how sorry I am. . . . It doesn't seem to come out."

"We'll have it sent to the cleaner," Carol said firmly. "Come with me, Lin; you can't stay in a damp dress like that. It's horribly purple stuff, isn't it? I'll find something for you to put on. We're pretty much of a size."

Linda followed Carol upstairs and into a room at the far end of the corridor. She thought, almost irrelevantly, that earlier in the evening she had wondered how Carol's room was furnished and wished she could see it, but she had never thought that she *would* see it . . . and under such circumstances. She looked around interestedly at the green walls, the creamy draperies with a tracery of green and yellow leaves; and at the yellow rug and the ottoman in deep blue, the hanging bookshelves and the cabinet of miniature wooden animals.

Carol flung open her closet. "I'd say take your pick," she said, running her hand over the row of dresses in cellophane bags, with little clusters of sachet attached to each hanger, "but I know you wouldn't. It was such a lovely dress," she mourned. Even in her absorption, Linda noticed that she hadn't said it was becoming—only that

175

it was a lovely dress. "I think I know the very thing for you," she went on, "if it fits, and it ought to."

She pulled out a severely simple crepe-backed satin—white blouse with long, full sleeves gathered into tight cuffs; a wide, crushed cherry-red girdle; a long, supple black skirt. Linda felt a rush of disappointment. Beggars couldn't be choosers, of course; but it would have been fun to try on one of the other fascinating dresses she glimpsed in the closet.

"Put it on. . . . Here, I'll help you get out of this." The tiered net fell to the floor in a little heap, which Carol deftly gathered up and spread over a hanger, and the satin slipped over her head; fell, almost miraculously, into place on her body. "It fits as if it were made for you!" Carol cried. "Oh, Linda, look at yourself! Isn't it stunning on you? It was *made* for you."

It was true. Linda could scarcely believe her eyes. It didn't seem possible that a dress could make such a difference in her appearance. She felt as if she had undergone a complete metamorphosis . . . and she liked the result. There before her in the long mirror stood the kind of person she had always wanted to be. It was queer that she had never been able to achieve it by herself. But Carol had unerringly chosen the right sheath for her. Her neck looked longer, so that her head sat well. The creamy white brought out the color in her skin and even lent light to her hair. The long sleeves made her arms look less long; the prominent wristbones were hidden, and the hands seemed smaller. The fullness of the blouse made
176

her shoulders narrower; and the material was immensely becoming to her figure, softening some lines and accenting others.

Carol grabbed her by the hand. "Come down and let me show off my creation! I'm terribly proud of you!"

Flying down the stairs with her hostess, Linda still had time to think, "I've always admired Carol—the way she looks, the way she acts. It's funny I never realized that she and I are pretty much the same type, tall and long-limbed and with big bones. Carol knew how to bring out her good points, I suppose, and I didn't. That made all the difference."

The way the others greeted her entry was flattering, to say the least. It was almost as if, with the changing of dresses, she had changed personalities. And they liked this new person she had become. They seemed to think of her as a different person—someone new and really quite interesting.

One or two of the girls were outspoken. "Why, Linda, where have *you* been hiding?" And Sue Hapgood cried, striking an exaggerated pose, "It isn't fair! Two changes in one evening . . . and maybe more to come. Buzz, spill some punch on me!"

The rest of the evening passed like a dream, a happy dream that left her excited and smiling and not wanting to wake up.

"Ben's seeing you home," Carol said at last.

And, though she knew it must have been arranged, that made Linda happy, too.

177

"It was a *lovely* party," she said warmly, gratitude and pleasure coloring her voice. "I don't know when I've had such a good time. It was sweet of you to ask me."

Carol said, "I wanted to right away. But then I heard about your sister. . . . And when Ginny Martin dropped out, I thought of you first thing. You were a peach to be such a good sport about it."

Linda felt suddenly at peace. The inner thing that had been bothering her all evening—and ever since the invitation—was all smoothed out. Carol hadn't tried to hide the fact that she had asked Linda at the last minute; she took it for granted that Linda knew and understood. And she had said that she wanted to ask her in the beginning. That made Linda feel warm and pleasant inside. In spite of Helen Walters, she believed her. She found that it was much easier to believe Carol than Helen. Helen had a way of distorting the truth just enough to cast doubt on everything that happened, so that you were distrustful and confused. She'd been a fool to listen to Helen against her own convictions. Well, she wouldn't any more. She was free of Helen and all her sly innuendoes and nasty little cracks.

Ben said, as they plodded through the scrunchy snow, "I'm glad you're rid of that reform bunch, Linda."

It was almost as if he had read her thoughts. "I am, too," she said.

"They aren't your kind," he said. "And you aren't theirs."

"I found that out," she said humbly.

178

Well, she *had* found it out . . . no use telling him how. Sometimes the truth had to be crammed down your throat, as this had been. She had to be thrown out on her ear before she realized what she was being saved from. But it had happened, and she was glad.

She said now, curiously, "Does everybody know about the club? They seemed to think they were pretty secret."

He scoffed. "Sure, everybody knows about it—including Mr. Galbraith. They're a bunch of malcontents. It stands to reason they'd try to get together. Nobody else wants them around, so they herd together. And they'll get tired of each other pretty soon, too." He guided her between two high drifts and over a slippery bit of pavement. "You know, Linda," he said then, "I never can get over the queer way some people go about things. Gosh knows there's plenty of things that need reforming—even here in school—but getting off in a huddle and beefing about it isn't going to change it. Why not come out in the open? Stand up in meeting and say what you think? Bring it out in the air. The way they act you'd think they were afraid to have their honest resentment looked at or torn to bits. If you have a conviction you ought to be able to stand by it, fight for it if necessary."

"Yes," she said.

He was putting into words what she had felt—at first vaguely, then with growing strength. It was what she had tried to tell them, but they had rudely silenced her.

"It's like this war," he went on. "Maybe you don't approve of the way every little thing's being done, but it's

179

the big idea behind it. That's what you want to be a part of and fight for. Working *with* it, we'll get it done; standing off and grousing about the big shots and rationing and gas shortage and stuff just holds it back . . . and makes you darn unpopular besides. Did you ever notice that not one of those Reform Clubbers—not *one* of 'em —is in any school activity or community group? They don't want to work with, only against. They're sourpusses, that's all. If they don't snap out of it they'll be that way all through life."

Linda said, with new confidence, "I feel as if I'd had a narrow escape!"

He laughed. "I'll say you did! It was about time somebody of us drew lots to tell you where you got off. But you were smart; you got off yourself." Linda kept silent, but he did not seem to notice. "I guess I've been to blame, too. I should have put you to work for us. Only, you know how it is—there were so many things to get started and organized, I sort of got lost in the maze. And when I had to think of somebody I naturally thought of those I'd tried out before—ones I knew I could count on. . . . But the Victory Corps will be getting started, and with a bang, right after New Year's. Mr. Galbraith told me so. That'll put us all to work. You'll be up to your ears, I guess."

"That suits me," she said happily.

They were almost home; she looked through the tree branches outlined against the sky and saw lights all over the lower floor, and in Amy's room upstairs. All at once
180

her happiness fled; terror took its place. Something had happened! Amy was ill again—perhaps had had a relapse. She broke into a run, Ben beside her.

With her heart pounding uncomfortably, she was hunting for her key when the door was opened. "Bob, what is it? What's happened?"

Bob's face broke into an excited grin. "Boy, are we celebrating! Jinks is back, and Dad sent a telegram saying he's coming home tomorrow to spend Christmas with us!"

Linda threw off her coat, laughing with happiness and relief. "Oh, that's wonderful!" she cried.

Bob was staring at her. "Well, for Pete's sake, what happened to *you?*"

She looked down; she had forgotten, for the moment, that she was wearing Carol's dress.

"I'll tell you later," she said impatiently. She read the telegram for herself, and then demanded, "You tell *me* about Jinks. How . . . who . . . when . . ."

"I was sitting here reading." Bob relished the chance to tell the story that he had been saving all evening. "It was pretty late, but I thought—you know—I ought to stay up in case. Well, in case. The bell rang and I went, and there was a kid—about my age, I guess—and he looked pretty scared but sort of determined, and he had Jinks on a string. Jinks nearly knocked him down trying to get in the house, but the kid wouldn't let go till he told his story. Seems he saw the write-up in the paper tonight —all about how Amy was still sick and wouldn't get better till her dog came home—and he decided he'd better get square with himself or he wouldn't enjoy Christmas. So he brought Jinks back. I felt sort of sorry for him, because he was crazy about the dog—you could see that— and he said he'd never had one, and Jinks just came to his door that night and was hungry and he fed him and then tied him up. He knew Jinks belonged to us, but he kept telling himself every day he'd bring him back; only he couldn't. But Christmas got him, and it's a good thing, too," Bob said sternly. "I told him if he wanted a dog he could get one, like we did, for fifty cents at the pound. Only not so good as Jinks."

"Happy ending, all right," Ben said. "Well, no need to wish you a merry Christmas; but I do."

"And to you, Ben," Linda said softly.

She went upstairs then and peeped into Amy's room. Amy was asleep, a half-smile on her face; and in her arms—asleep, too—lay a contented wire-haired terrier. There were pawmarks on the rug and on the spread, but Linda ignored them. She crossed the room on tiptoe and turned out the light.

CHAPTER TEN

LINDA, leaving her galoshes on the mat, gave a quick rat-tat-tat on Mrs. Clayborne's back door and then went in, as she had been told to do. In the kitchen she stopped short. There were voices—Mrs. Clayborne's and a man's low, unhurried one. Company . . . perhaps she'd better slip out as quickly as she had come.

"What are you doing—stealing cookies? Come on in; I hear you!" Mary Clayborne called from the doorway. Linda had never seen her look so happy and animated. Behind her stood a tall young man in uniform. "Surprise, surprise!" Mary Clayborne said excitedly. "Jerrold popped in on me—forty-eight hours' leave. Isn't that the most marvelous New Year's present? Linda, this is my pride and joy. And Jerrold—"

"I've heard enough about you to know that this is none other than Linda Marsh," he said pleasantly, holding out his hand.

He was like the photographs that stood on mantel and table, and on Mrs. Clayborne's vanity. Only better-looking. He was tanned and his white teeth sparkled in his brown face. Lean and muscular, with a shock of sandy-brown hair. Impeccable uniform and an infectious smile. She liked him at once. No wonder Mrs. Clayborne was so proud, couldn't take her eyes from him.

Over tea they got acquainted. He was easy to talk to.

"I've been trying to get all the news, and a bit of gossip (man-style, you know) out of Mother; but she's absolutely no good. All she wants to know is whether I have enough blankets at night and how I get such a high shine on my shoes, and what the General said to me at dinner—"

"Jerrold, you bold, bad fibber! Is that what Army life has done to you?" his mother demanded, going into the kitchen for hot water.

He grinned back. "And worse. Maybe Linda can help me out."

"We're so new here I don't know much news, and the same goes for gossip," she returned. "And, besides, I'd rather hear you talk. I never met an Army flier before, and I'd love to hear—"

He threw up his hands. "Don't tell me I'll be driven from home. I absolutely refuse to talk about myself or camp. If you two can't come across with something else, we'll play silence."

"Oh, Linda, Linda," Mrs. Clayborne whispered in the pantry. All the gaiety and happiness were wiped from her face. "I'm afraid this leave means he's going overseas. He won't say and I daren't ask. . . . I can't bear it!"

Then, to Linda's amazement, the animation was put back; her voice had its familiar lilt, and she went into the living room head high and smiling.

184

"Darling, I've an idea. We'll throw a little party, very informal, and ask all your old friends that we can get hold of. And you can ply them with questions to your heart's content. It will be fun. Linda will help, won't you, Linda?"

"Of course! When do we start?"

"This very minute. We'll ask them for tonight. And, Jerrold, you sit there and think whom you'd like to have and what you want to eat."

"Don't bother with a party, Mother. You're the only girl I want and, as for fellows—I'm fed up with them at camp."

"Don't bother to be polite, Jerrold. You're the most social person I know. Now hurry; we haven't a minute to waste. . . . Linda, do you think we could rustle up some tongue and bologna, and what sort of salad would you have?"

It was as simple as that. As naturally as if she belonged in the family, Linda was drawn into the impromptu plans. Under her competent suggestions the menu took shape; Jerrold was at the telephone, laughing at his friends' surprise that he was in town, taking with pleased nonchalance their vociferous acceptances for the party.

"Mrs. Clayborne," he announced, between chats, "your son is a popular boy. They're flocking to the call."

"It's the table your mother sets," she retorted, "and don't forget it for a minute."

"Between us, anyhow, we're irresistible."

"And whatever horrible report Linda gives to her

185

father will be on your shoulders, you conceited creature." Mrs. Clayborne had the last word.

At six-thirty Linda gave a final look of inspection at the trays of thin-sliced buttered bread, the platters of cold meat, the stuffed eggs and relishes, the pot of beans simmering in the oven, and flew home to dress. At seven she was back again, flushed and excited.

"How does it look?" she demanded of Mrs. Clayborne. "You helped me choose it. . . . But does it still look all right?"

"Perfect, my dear!"

They had shopped together for the new formal. Linda, afire with her recent discovery, had imparted it to Mrs. Clayborne, and her neighbor had said, "I'm so glad you found it out. You're a different type, Linda, and you ought to be proud of it. Not run-of-the-mill pretty; not ordinary good looks. But a kind that sets you apart and ought to be respected and played up. Oh, it's difficult— I'll admit that! Being tall and broad-shouldered and having long arms and legs doesn't make it easy to find the right clothes for you. But you see it *can* be done. And the result ought to thrill you. It does me."

With Mary Clayborne's help, then, she had chosen a suit—soft gray flannel, tailored and trim; some blouses to go with it, and a sweater. The tiered net formal had been disposed of at the Utility Shop. "I don't want it around," Linda said stoutly. Not that she would be tempted to wear it, ever again; but she felt that with her new clothes a new life was beginning, and she wanted it all of one piece. Mrs. Clayborne had helped her build this fresh picture of herself—the tailored girl, tall, distinguished, a little different from the rest and proud of it.

Mary Clayborne had said shrewdly, "Everybody ought to know himself; to take pride in his individuality. After all, that's the only thing that makes us stand out from other people. If you realize your good points and feature them, and know your bad points as well and tone them down, you get a new conception of yourself. It helps you carry your body, and it helps you in your relationship with others. You stop being envious of the type you've always admired . . . and it does something to you to know that people who aren't 'on to themselves' yet are envying *you* and wishing they looked like you and could dress like you."

Linda thought, a little guiltily, of the thousand times she had sighed over some petite girl's fragile prettiness; over some friend's new hair-do, or a girl's fluffy, frilly dress. How she had longed for furbelows that weren't becoming to her; how she had deliberately covered her attractive points by dressing unsuitably . . . merely because she carried someone else's image in her mind, instead of her own.

The Utility Shop had paid her an outright sum for the tiered net. Not anywhere near its original cost, she thought ruefully, but enough to make her feel she could spend money on a new dress. And her Christmas check had come in beautifully for the suit and blouses. These things would do to start her off, and from now on, she vowed, her monthly allowance would be spent with "the tailored girl" in mind. She didn't doubt that she would still sometimes wish for something sheer and ruffly, something dainty and ultrafeminine; but she was also sure that she would be able to withstand it. And that was a triumph of a sort.

Just the same, she pirouetted in Mrs. Clayborne's kitchen and demanded, "Does it really look the way I hope it looks?"

She saw Mrs. Clayborne's eyes flicking over the bronze-green faille, falling in thick soft folds to her ankles; over the square neckline emphasized by two large plain gold clips; over the elbow-length sleeves, severely untrimmed, and the girdle of twisted green and gold.

"You look," she said deliberately, "exactly as I've always imagined you could look, and nothing could be higher praise than that. . . . Now here, if you insist on helping out, you must cover up with my largest apron. It would be tragedy if so much as a drop of mayonnaise fell on that creation!"

It was fun, all of it. The guests were people she didn't know, older than herself, but they were friendly and informal. The house was filled with talk and laughter; the food disappeared as if by magic; somebody played the piano while they sang rollicking and sentimental songs; Linda was introduced to half a dozen new games, foolish and mirth-provoking . . . and it wasn't until the candles had guttered low and the fire died on the hearth that any-one was disposed to go home.

"Now *that*," Jerrold said with immense satisfaction, "was an evening worth coming home for. Thanks, both of you, for a swell time."

"Don't thank me," Linda protested. "I was a guest, too. I'm dead on my feet, but it was worth it."

Mrs. Clayborne kissed her. "Now, not a bit of clearing or stacking. I'm going to bed and dream the dreams of the righteous. You were such a joy, Linda. I don't know what I would have done without you."

Brushing her long bob till it shone, Linda thought happily over the past five hours. It hadn't been just the hospitality of the Claybornes, or the good food, or the jolly friends, that had made the party such a success for her. It was largely the new dress, and her knowledge that she looked well in it.

Being sure of herself had made her, for almost the first time in her social life, forget her appearance completely. Inwardly she was serene, as outwardly she knew she was attractive. It gave her poise, and poise gave her charm. People had had a chance to know her for herself . . . they hadn't been stopped by her unsuitable clothes that gave her a false exterior. It was something of a circle; she wasn't sure that she had thought it out right, but the result had been all she could have asked for. It was queer what clothes could do to you . . . clothes and the right hair-do, a low, controlled voice, and the warm feeling that you were looking your best. It was queer—and rather wonderful, too. Because once you got "on to yourself" you had solved a major problem of your life.

Even Amy had recognized the difference at once. Her shrewd, knowing young eyes had lit approvingly.

"Now *that* dress looks like you," she had said, one arm around a contented Jinks. "That other one, too," she added, "that you had from Carol. They're your kind of clothes. Why didn't you ever—"

Linda had laughed. "I was a goon, that's all. But from now on watch me!"

She had no idea that she would see Jerrold Clayborne again—certainly not on such a brief furlough, when it was only natural that his mother would claim every minute of his time. But Sunday afternoon he came to the door.

"Do me a favor?" he asked, with his ingratiating grin.

"Of course," she said recklessly.

"Be careful!" he warned.

She amended, laughing, "Well, anything within reason."

"This isn't within reason," he said. "It's a whim, a momentary yearning, a sudden desire."

"Come in and meet the family," she said. "Bob's dying to know you—and Amy won't confess it, but she is, too. As for Dad—"

"He'll speak for himself, thank you," Mr. Marsh announced, coming from the living room, pipe in hand.

"I hope you aren't dying, too, sir," Jerrold said, extending his hand. He seemed to tower over Mr. Marsh, and the slight stoop to his figure as he bent to speak to him, and the way he spoke, gave him an attractively defer-
190

ential air. "I must say it's highly flattering, though, to have a whole family pining to meet me."

He spent fifteen minutes talking to Mr. Marsh, admiring Jinks, surviving Amy's concentrated stare, and answering Bob's rapid-fire questions. Then he turned to Linda.

"Don't let your nice family sidetrack me. I came with a purpose, and it's growing apace. I want to know if you'll go for a snow hike with me?"

"Now?"

"When else? I feel like a stretch, and you've no idea what a joy a snow scene like this is to me. I've been resting my jaundiced eyes on scrub pine and raggedy palms and sand stretches for so long I want to get a real case of snow blindness before I go back."

"You sound desperate," she said. "I suppose I'd better go with you, in case you get drunk on the beauty of the scene and forget to come home."

"Take a staff or two along—and maybe Jinks, with a keg of spirits around his neck. There's no telling where we'll end up."

Linda put on a short woolly coat and her red rubber boots, and set a tiny knitted calot on the back of her head. "Is that supposed to keep you warm?" Jerrold inquired with interest.

"No more so than an overseas cap," she returned.

"Overseas caps have a function," he reminded her with mock severity.

191

"And calots have, too," she laughed back at him. "They're conserving material for the war effort. Where shall we go?"

"Oh, anywhere," he said. "It doesn't matter. I just wanted to scuffle in the snow and at the same time have a talk with you."

"That's nice," she said, feeling pleased. "What about?"

"Not about the war," he answered quickly. "I want to forget it for two days. . . . Not that one can. And, in a way, what I want to talk about is tied up with the war, too. It touches everything; it touches everyone. It's changed our lives around, and I suppose we're foolish to try to forget it, even for a moment." They were walking rapidly down the road, staying in the street because it was easier going. "Let's cut across here," he suggested. "There's a field where we can wade in snow, if we like, and a grand view of the hills. There's a little brook, too— well, really a rill—where we can pretend we're skating."

When they were plodding desultorily across the field, making tracks in the snow and weaving a zigzag path for the pure fun of it, he said, "You're pretty fond of Mother, aren't you?"

Linda stopped short; her eyes met his.

"Fond of her!" she cried. "I love her. She's a darling. She was my first real friend when we moved to town and I was feeling terribly alone and—sort of frightened; and sometimes I think she's still the only real friend I have."

"I don't believe that," he said warmly. "But I saw how

much you thought of Mother, and you don't know how it bucked me up. Because she's keen about you."

He said it simply, with utter conviction. Linda didn't know why she should be so surprised and happy to hear that, but she was. She had never stopped to wonder how Mrs. Clayborne must feel toward her, thinking only that Mrs. Clayborne was being neighborly and kind—doing small and large services out of the goodness of her heart and her understanding of how bewildered and uncertain a newcomer like herself must be in the beginning.

She had taken Mrs. Clayborne's kindness for granted —gratefully, always; but she had never thought of it as being the expression of real affection for herself. Somehow, hearing this from her son, gave her unwonted pleasure.

She said now, "Oh . . . oh, I'd like to think so!"

He laughed at her solemn face. "Why, you funny kid! Don't you *know* it? Gosh, ever since you moved in next door Mother's letters have been full of you. She said you had grown to be more and more like a daughter to her. She thought of you that way, she said . . . as the daughter she never had, but always longed for."

Linda felt quick tears in her eyes; she whisked them away with her mittened hand, but not with shame. She was proud and humble, at the same time.

"I never had a nicer thing said to me," she whispered. "Never, in all my life."

"Mother doesn't take to everyone, either," he affirmed.

193

"You might not know it, but I do. She's a person of quick decisions—and surprisingly right, ninety times out of a hundred. If she likes you, she goes for you in a big way. If she doesn't, she—well, she doesn't!" He laughed. "Not many people have found out what it is not to be on Mrs. Clayborne's list, but the few who have have practically congealed!"

"I don't believe *that*," she retorted. "Your mother's the kindest, sweetest person I've ever known."

"Kind, yes," he admitted readily. "But not sweet. I mean, not the ordinary namby-pamby variety a person thinks of when he hears the word 'sweet.' But if it's a good quality she has it." He broke off and laughed boyishly. "I guess I'm pretty fond of her myself!" Then, as quickly, he sobered. "That's why I'm turning to you. I want your help."

"My help?" she repeated. "What do you mean?"

His boot made a half circle in the snow. He looked down at it, then up at her.

"To blurt it right out—I want you to promise to keep an eye on her."

"Keep an eye on her!"

She sounded like an echo, and not a very intelligent one, but she couldn't help it. He didn't seem to notice.

"Yes. You know—run in often and see how she's getting on, how she's bearing up with me away. . . . I may be going far away," he said slowly. "One of these days. Maybe soon." Linda thought swiftly of Mrs. Clayborne's anguished words in the pantry. Then she had suspected the truth. "I'm not telling," Jerrold said, "because, after all, I don't know. No one knows just when or how. But it's on the books. And I'd be a lot happier, a lot easier in my mind, if I felt that somebody who cared about Mother was keeping an eye on her . . . seeing that she was all right, that she wasn't lonely. Somebody who'd know if she was ill. Somebody who'd write me a letter now and then and tell me—just on the q.t., you know—the absolute truth. Mothers never tell the truth about themselves." He grinned. "That's why I thought of you . . . after I heard about you from Mother, and particularly after I met you and saw for myself what you thought of her." He looked at her intently. "So—would you? Would it be too much to ask?"

"Of course I'll do it," she said warmly. "I'd love to. And I'm awfully proud you think I'm the person to do it."

He held out his hand and she put hers in it.

"It's a bargain, then. And thanks no end. What a load off my chest! . . . It isn't," he said whimsically, "that I think Mother can't look after herself—heaven knows she's been doing it long enough, and without too much thought from me—but being away, even just down at camp, makes a fellow wonder a lot what's going on at home. Mother wouldn't tell if anything went wrong; she'd keep it to herself and try to struggle through. But with you giving me the low-down, and with your family next door to pop in on her and keep her cheerful, I'll do a much better job. And"—he hesitated, and for the first time some of his assurance deserted him—"there's another thing. Am I asking too much?"

"I don't know what it is till you tell me," Linda answered. "But so far it's just a privilege."

"Thanks," his smile flashed back. "The rest is this: When you're writing, don't make it all about Mother. I mean—don't think you have to give me just a detailed account of her doings. I'd like to hear about you, too. You and your family. Anything you want to write. A fellow likes to get letters when he's far from home. People don't realize it, I guess, because, no matter how good friends they are, they don't write very often. And some of them are the—the darnedest letter writers! Short, and not even to the point! You get hungry for home news, and little incidents, and a bit of humor now and then . . . even if the writer has to make it up. . . . Are you a good letter writer?"

Linda laughed. "I don't know. But I do know I'll try— for you. I'll save all the scraps of news and dress them up in my best style. Particularly since you don't seem to care whether it's the truth or not so long as it's interesting!"

"I'll spot the truth all right," he prophesied. "Come on, we've got to celebrate a major victory . . . for me. Let's go down to the Dainty Shoppe and have ourselves a dish of something special."

Linda felt elated and proud. Jerrold had honored her by his request. It meant that he trusted her, because his mother loved her. And he had said that his mother did not like everyone indiscriminately. She couldn't help being thrilled, too, that he didn't just want news of Mother . . . but of her, and of her family. He thought she'd make an interesting correspondent. He had chosen her, out of all the people he knew, to be a sort of liaison officer between him and the home front. She walked, tall and erect, before him into the steamy atmosphere of the Dainty Shoppe.

Helen Walters was sitting by herself in a corner, humped over a chocolate malted.

"Hello, Helen," Linda said cheerily.

Helen rolled her eyes upward, still sucking at the straw; she looked directly at Linda, and beyond.

"The cut direct, if ever I saw one," Jerrold said with an exaggerated shiver, when they were seated. "What brings that on?"

"A little private battle." Linda was surprised at her own airiness. It didn't hurt her, as once it might have. Now it was amusing. Helen was being childish. "War's in the air these days."

"Anything I can do?" he asked.

"Just order a double vanilla-raspberry to keep my spirits up," she retorted merrily.

How far she had come from Helen and the Reform Club in just this short time! She felt, somehow, that with the holidays a new life was opening out for her. She didn't know what course it would take, or whether she was perhaps just being foolishly cheerful, because her

197

desires were so strong to have it that way. But the feeling persisted, and lent her wings. She was glad that she had spoken to Helen. There was not even room for rancor in this new life . . . whatever it was to be.

When school began again, early in January, she made a point of hunting up Jane Griggs at once.

"You must understand how it is, Jane," she said earnestly. "I don't want to hound you, or hurry you too much; but there's such a need for these things, and, besides, my quota is long past due. I kept holding it up so I could include your sweater and have it complete."

"I don't know what you're talking about," Jane said blandly. "I never did a sweater for you."

"You *promised* to do one," Linda corrected. "I suppose the holidays have been pretty busy for everybody. Still—"

"I didn't promise, either," Jane stated flatly.

Linda was openmouthed. "Why, Jane, surely you haven't forgotten in this short time! Don't you remember —I gave you four hanks of khaki wool, and I lent you a pair of needles until you could buy some. You said—"

Jane said, "Listen, I haven't got all day to stand here. You're nuts. I never got any wool from you—or needles, for that matter—and I certainly never said I'd do a sweater. I've plenty of other things to do without getting balled up with a lot of yarn. So skip it, will you?"

And, to Linda's horror, she pushed past and down the corridor, her short plaid skirt switching perkily.

Linda thought, "I must be dreaming. How can she say a thing like that? Has she lost her memory? Why, I can see the incident as clearly as I can see these walls."

What was she to do now? If Jane denied ever receiving materials from her, she certainly would never produce a sweater. And if Linda didn't have the sweater, she would have failed in her promise to the Red Cross. It would put her in wrong with Mrs. Wing. It would probably mean the end of the whole project if headquarters felt they couldn't count on her for such a simple thing as turning in completed articles for a specified amount of wool.

She realized, with a sinking heart, that, whereas she had signed at headquarters for the wool, she hadn't anything to show how much she had given individual knitters, or the date. She had trusted them, and she had trusted her own memory. Everyone else had turned in her garment as agreed. She had certainly never visualized a possibility like this—that one of the girls would deny ever having received the wool.

The incident troubled her; she kept revolving the question of what to do around and around in her mind. The simplest thing, of course, she decided, would be to go to headquarters and make a clean breast of the matter.

Mrs. Wing listened gravely.

"I'm more than willing to pay for the wool," Linda said anxiously. "It's my fault that there's been this mix-up—"

"It isn't simply a matter of paying," Mrs. Wing interrupted. "The cost of the wool itself is a trifling part of it. It's keeping our records straight that is important. Are you sure, my dear, that you gave Jane Griggs the necessary wool?"

"Absolutely sure, Mrs. Wing," Linda said earnestly. "I know the amount and the date. . . . I just haven't anything down in black and white to show for it."

"Well," Mrs. Wing said a little wearily, "I suppose I had better telephone Jane Griggs myself, and see if we can't straighten it out. Meanwhile, I'm glad you brought the other garments in. They look very nice," she said, inspecting them with a critical eye and noting how professionally they had been blocked and labeled. "But I can't give you anything further to work on until this business is cleared up. You understand that, don't you?"

"Yes," Linda said. There was a lump in her throat. It hurt to be taken to task, however gently; to be thought remiss and careless. Not to be trusted any more. She must get the truth out of Jane—she must! "If you get any word from Jane, Mrs. Wing, won't you please let me know?" she begged. "I'm—I'm more anxious than you, I think, to have it straightened out."

"I'll let you know," Mrs. Wing promised, but there was a formal note in her voice that hadn't been there before.

Linda couldn't blame her. She could only go on the evidence, and the evidence was that there was a sweater missing for which she had given out wool. Some of Linda's new-found confidence evaporated with this interview, leaving her uncertain and a little afraid.

Mrs. Parsons was highly indignant when she heard of the complication.

"The idea!" she snorted. "The very idea! What do they think you did—ate it? You go down and buy me some of that khaki wool at the store. I'll give you the money, and I'll knit you a sweater to make up for that Griggs girl!"

"Why, Mrs. Parsons," Linda cried, very much touched and not a little startled, "you don't need to do a thing like that! And you don't like to knit on big things, anyhow."

"So I don't," Mrs. Parsons came back promptly, with a toss of her head, "but that's beside the point. I can knit on 'em as well as the next one. I'm not going to have you being accused of something you never done."

"Well, it's sweet of you," Linda said warmly. "But I hope you won't have to. I'll wait a bit, first, and see what happens."

The school hummed with activity. The Victory Corps had been set up and was now functioning. Junior and Senior boys were taking precommando training that occupied much of their time after school hours. Girls were inducted into various special courses that would fit them for wartime service.

Linda was urged to join the nutrition class. She laughed.

201

"Thanks, but that's one I could almost teach myself! I've had to do so much planning and buying, and making things do on a small budget, that I know quite a few tricks. Mother was wonderful about that—she always made me plan for proteins and carbohydrates, and look after calories and the proper number of green and yellow vegetables, and that sort of thing. And I think my family's a pretty good indication of how well Mother's nutrition course took!"

She volunteered, instead, for service at the Day Nursery two afternoons a week, taking care of some of the small children left there by working mothers, entertaining them, preparing their midafternoon snacks, and seeing that they had the proper rest and play. The Day Nursery was overcrowded; the directress complained that the children hung out of the windows and bulged the walls, but she could not refuse to take a new one and, as a result, the staff was unable to cope with the overflow. Women from various organizations took turns with the Junior League and older girls from the high school in helping to care for the children, and Linda was sure that her training in looking after Amy and Bob would stand her in good stead here.

Early in the month the school bulletin board announced: "The Junior-Senior Feed is a tradition we won't give up! Come to the meeting, Juniors, and help us plan it!" Linda went, curious to know what would be done this year. There was a kind of easygoing rivalry in seeing if each new Junior class couldn't top the efforts

202

of the previous one in entertaining the Seniors. Linda had heard fabulous tales of other spreads.

There had been some talk of forgoing the feast this year because of the war, but she was glad it hadn't been given up after all. There were plenty of ways to circumvent shortages, and it seemed to her that a traditional thing like that shouldn't lightly be omitted. She was full of cooperative spirit when she entered the library, where the meeting was to be held. She was sure she could be of service—there were lots of ways in which she could help, and no doubt everyone would have to fall to and do his share to make it the kind of success it ought to be.

It would be fun to work for something as personal and —well, selfish as this Junior-Senior Feed. There had been so much concentration on war work and war efforts that a great deal of the school's carefree spirit had been absorbed in more serious concerns. They were entitled to this one spree when they could get together without a serious aim.

Linda saw that Edith Merrick was in charge of the committee on arrangements. She looked around for Carol and Ben, but neither was present.

"Ben's at a salvage meeting," Myra whispered, just before the gavel fell, "and Carol's home with a twisted ankle . . . skating."

Edith was in her element. She had the chair; there was excitement in the air; she was in command of the performance, and she acted the part. Linda noticed all this without giving it too much thought. It was too bad that

203

the Drama Club had been given up, though. She had looked forward to being invited to join after the play. But they had decided that the time spent in rehearsals and productions could be put to better advantage these days, and the Drama Club was out for the duration. Oh well, Linda thought, with only a momentary pang of regret, there were other things now.

"I have grand news," Edith announced, almost at once. She knew how to catch their interest. "I knew you'd want me to go ahead, since I was in charge, but of course if you don't approve we can always change. Only it was too good a chance to miss . . . and I do think you'll be awfully pleased."

"Tell all, Edith. Our hearts are weak," someone called out.

"You'll revive, then, when you hear this: I got Christiansen to promise to do the catering! Isn't that marvelous!"

Whistles of surprise, of unbelief, of approbation. "Gosh, but isn't he expensive? We'll be broke for seven years!"

Edith preened. "That's the best part. He said he'd do it for a special price. Practically cost. His daughter went to Brookhaven High, you know."

They clamored for details. The menu was simple, the price fairly high; but no one demurred. It would be rather swanky to have Christiansen cater . . . he did it for all the best parties in town; and everybody knew what swell sandwiches he made, and his angel cakes and ice creams were tops. It would take a lot off their hands, too, they agreed.

"That's exactly what I felt," Edith said with pride. "We won't have to worry about the food, so we can concentrate on decorations and the entertainment and the dance. Now, this is what I thought . . ."

Linda admitted that Edith had thought it all out pretty well. She rattled off committees, naming chairmen then and there and asking them to give her a tentative list of their other members at once from among those present. There was a job to suit everybody's special talent, Linda noticed. Everett Gore, of course, in charge of the music. Sam Hellburn, who was good at organizing, to take care of individual invitations and acceptances. Kathy Joost, whose father was a florist, for the floral arrangements. Myra to decorate the tables and the hall. Gene Trumbull for getting ushers and floormen for the dance. She whisked through the list, handing out duties as favors, and everyone grinned happily at his particular job. The list was almost done.

"Oh yes," Edith said, looking up, starry-eyed, "I forgot one thing. Christiansen said we could use the cafeteria dishes; that would save us a lot. But of course *we'll* have to take care of the dishwashing."

Groans. "Count me out." . . . "I get enough at home." . . . "Let's have paper plates!"

"Now *who*," said Edith, "will I put in charge of that? Be still a minute; I can't think." They quieted temporarily, and in the silence Edith pretended to think. "I have it!" she said then, brightly. "The very person for the dirty work . . . Linda Marsh!"

Linda felt a slow flush mounting to her hair; her heart hammered furiously. That was nasty. It wasn't fair. She forced her hot eyes to look around at her classmates. It wasn't going down so well with them. The dig was a little too obvious, too unkind . . . they felt it, but the silence lengthened and no one spoke. No one objected; no one came to her defense. Edith sat staring straight at her with a triumphant half-smile. This was paying her back with a vengeance! This would put Linda Marsh in her place.

"I won't be a worm," Linda thought angrily. "Now's my chance to show them what I'm made of. If I let them get away with this, my name might as well be Mud from now on."

She rose slowly to her feet. She forced her lips into a semblance of a curve. "Remember your voice," she said to herself sternly. "Don't let it sound like a whine—not now, not now!"

"All right," she said. "I accept with pleasure. Somebody has to do the dishes, and they won't be dirty when *I* get through with them."

It was the hardest thing she had ever done. She had chosen to ignore Edith's innuendo and had taken her words at their face value. She had forced herself to rise and make them focus their attention on her. Her knees trembled with the effort of supporting her while she waited for their reaction.

206

It came with a rush. The silence was shattered by their vociferous applause.

"Atta girl, Linda!" Buzz cried.

And, surprisingly, Dana poked her in the back. "You're a good sport, Linda," she said. "You can count on me to help you."

CHAPTER ELEVEN

AFTER the meeting a number of them gathered around her.

"That was a mean crack," they said. "You were pretty decent about it, Linda."

They made her feel warm and welcome. Edith was ostentatiously busy at the far end of the room, not ever glancing in their direction. She did not look quite so smug and vindictively smiling now. She realized that she had played her scene wrong, that she had lowered her rating with her classmates. It was triumph of a sort for Linda.

But it didn't last long.

When she got home Mrs. Parsons said, "Mrs. Wing called you up. Said you was to come down to the Red Cross rooms as soon as you could. It was important, she said."

Linda's heart sank. It might have been good news, but somehow she was afraid it was not. If it had been good, surely Mrs. Wing would have left some reassuring message with Mrs. Parsons.

She grabbed up her mittens again and hurried down to headquarters.

"Have you heard from Jane Griggs?" she inquired breathlessly.

Mrs. Wing looked grave. "Yes, I have. And I must say I don't like this new development at all."

"What did she say?"

"She said she had no wool from you and made no promise to knit for you. Just what you told me she said. But she claims that it was possible you had used the wool yourself."

"I?" Linda was aghast.

"To knit something for a soldier friend of yours . . . a gift which perhaps you gave him directly."

"Oh, how dare she!" Linda cried. Her eyes flashed angrily and two flags of color flew in her cheeks. "How dare she say a thing like that?"

"It seems she saw you with a soldier recently—"

"With a soldier!" Linda began a denial.

"In the Dainty Shoppe, wasn't it?"

"Oh . . . oh yes! But that was Jerrold Clayborne, the son of my next-door neighbor! I'd only met him that week end." Jane must have been present in the crowded shop. Or perhaps Helen had told her. "She doesn't think . . . Mrs. Wing," Linda said desperately, *"you* don't think—you don't believe I would do such a thing?"

"I don't want to believe it, Linda." Mrs. Wing was serious. "But I have only her word against yours. For the sake of all of us, and for the sake of the organization, I must have something more concrete than that. I should hate to think anything so petty of you . . . and I

209

shall be only too happy to have you disprove it. But until it *is* disproved . . ." She shrugged. "You must see my position, too, my dear."

"I do," Linda said miserably. Then her shoulders straightened. "And I'm going to clear this up if it's the last thing I do!"

She rounded up several of her knitting group on whose veracity she felt she could count.

"Did any of you see me give wool to Jane Griggs?" she demanded.

No one had.

"Well, did any of you ever see her knitting on Red Cross stuff?"

They shook their heads.

"It seems to me," Dana said, "that she made quite a point of telling how busy she was—so popular and all that—that she didn't have time for stodgy knitting."

"I know," Lillian nodded. "I heard that line a couple of times myself."

They looked blankly from one to the other.

"What's the huddle?" Sue asked from the doorway. She had come late, and they told her. "Did you ever see Jane knitting?" they chorused.

"Nope," she returned positively. Then, with an uptoss of her head, "Hey, wait a minute! I never saw her knit . . . but she must knit, because way last month, when I'd finished my sweater and was going to turn in the wool I had left—about a quarter of a ball, I guess—she stopped me one day and asked if I'd mind letting her have just a

210

little bit; she needed only a couple of yards or so. She was in an awful hurry, and I had it with me; so I unwound what she said was enough and broke it off and gave it to her. I turned the rest in. . . . Didn't I, Lin?"

"Yes," Linda nodded. "I remember."

"I didn't think anything of it at the time, and I didn't tell Linda about giving Jane that little wool because I didn't think it mattered . . . it really *was* only a couple of yards."

Linda said hopefully, "Did she say it was to finish a sweater?"

"No, she just said she needed a little wool."

It wasn't much to go on, but Linda reported her findings to Mrs. Wing. She had asked the girls not to say anything to Jane, because she wanted to work this thing out herself, and they had promised.

Mrs. Wing listened with a thoughtful air. Linda did not dare suggest what was in her own mind. She waited breathlessly while Mrs. Wing toyed with a pencil, making abstracted little marks on a white sheet of paper in front of her.

Suddenly she said, "Would you mind waiting, Linda, while I call Jane Griggs and ask her to come down here? I'd like to have you stay in the other room while I talk to her . . . it shouldn't take long, and there are some magazines there you might like to look over."

She closed the door—but not tightly, Linda noticed. When she heard Jane's rather heavy footsteps and high light voice, she got up restlessly. No magazine story

211

could hold her while this was going on. She listened shamelessly. She rather thought Mrs. Wing had meant that she should listen.

Mrs. Wing's voice was serious but pleasant as she greeted Jane.

"Such a bother for you to come down again," she said. "But I'm sure you don't mind answering a question or two for me."

"No, of course not," Jane said with assurance.

"There are several things I want to get straight in my mind. I think you said, Jane, that Linda Marsh never gave you wool?"

"That's right."

"In fact, you told me that you didn't knit at all."

"Yes."

There was a little pause.

Then Mrs. Wing said suddenly and clearly, "Then why, Jane, did you ask Sue Hapgood for some of her wool?"

"Why, I never—that is, I don't see— How did you—"

She was confused. Linda's heart pumped madly with hope.

Mrs. Wing continued firmly, "Was it, perhaps, to finish the sweater you were to make for the Red Cross so that you could send it, instead, to your cousin Frank Tobias?"

Linda was startled. How did Mrs. Wing know that? *She* didn't know that Jane had a cousin Frank Tobias.

Jane was silent, marshaling her forces possibly.

"You do have a cousin in the Army," Mrs. Wing said. It was a statement, not a question. "Stationed at Camp Bragg." Jane must have nodded dumbly, for Mrs. Wing continued, "We know that. And he has visited frequently at your house. We know that, too. You sent the sweater to him. Didn't you?"

Linda strained her ears for the answer. It came finally —a frightened, breathless little "Yes."

Mrs. Wing said, "Why, Jane?"

After an endless moment Jane answered. "I'll tell you why. I wanted to send Frank a Christmas present. He knows lots of girls, and I wanted my present to be something special. I never had any money to spend, and Dad won't give me an allowance, and Mother thought it was crazy to spend five dollars on Frank. . . . So I made up my mind I'd make the sweater for him. It was going to the Red Cross anyway, and they would have sent it to the Army. It didn't seem very wrong. Just—just quicker. And Frank said it was a wonderful sweater, and wrote the nicest letter about it."

Mrs. Wing said gently, "I can understand your wanting to make a special gift to your cousin, Jane. But wasn't it terribly unkind to Linda to have done that? Didn't you stop to think what it would mean to her reputation if this hadn't come out? And to put the blame on her for the very thing you had done yourself . . . surely that was not only unkind but unfair."

"Yes," Jane mumbled, so low that Linda could scarcely hear her. "I guess I just didn't think . . . and then when

213

she kept asking and asking me . . . I didn't know what to say . . . and it got worse, and finally—well, I just said maybe she did it."

Mrs. Wing got up and opened the door.

"Come in, Linda," she said. "I think Jane wants to tell you how sorry she is."

"Yes," Jane said hurriedly. "Yes, I do. I'm sorry things got so messed up, Linda."

"Possibly Linda would like you to do some little thing for her, to make up in a measure for the discomfort you've caused her."

Linda felt uncomfortable, but she saw the justice of the request. Jane would feel better if she did something in expiation.

"Well—I do need some helpers on my dishwashing committee," she said, with a small grin. "How about it, Jane?"

"All right . . . all right, I'll help. . . . Can I go now, Mrs. Wing?"

When she had scurried out, Linda said gratefully, "Oh, I'm so *glad* it's all cleared up. I felt as if I were going around with a weight on my chest and a band around my head."

Mrs. Wing nodded. "I feel the same way. And now that you're here, Linda, would you like to take along your next quota of wool?"

Linda said eagerly that she would. "And after this, I'm going to have a little card-index system and write down everything I give out and make every girl sign on

214

the dotted line for whatever she receives," she said firmly. "I don't want to go through *this* again!"

Her days grew increasingly full. Work at school had been pushed forward to make up for the extra-long winter vacation they had had and to crowd in additional courses that the war program made necessary. Keeping up with rationing edicts gave Linda plenty to ponder over, and she felt that to evolve interesting menus without an increased budget was not only a duty but a distinct feather in her cap.

"I'll be glad to raise you whenever you say the word," her father told her.

But she said proudly, "Not yet. I'm going to keep on this way as long as I can. It's a sort of challenge. And if I see any of you getting droopy or anemic I'll call for more money."

She was keeping an eye on Mrs. Clayborne, too, as she had promised Jerrold. Inviting her in to supper and for a game of Monopoly afterward. Dropping in occasionally, with her knitting, for a quiet hour by the fire and news of her son, who, miraculously, was still kept at camp. Including her in some of their movie parties, with stops at the Dainty Shoppe for a soda. She fitted into their plans with natural ease and always seemed very happy to be included. "She must have been really lonely before," Linda thought musingly. Somehow, she hadn't thought of Mrs. Clayborne as being lonely. But Jerrold had been right. He knew how much his mother

215

needed this inclusion in a family circle, how it brightened and made bearable her days.

A number of times Mary Clayborne was inveigled into playing chess with Mr. Marsh. She protested at first, saying she was rusty and hadn't been any good in the first place.

But afterward her father said admiringly, "By Jove, Lin, she's not only an attractive woman, but she can talk well *and* think well. I tell you I had to keep hopping to beat her when I did! One of these days she'll checkmate me—and in the classic three moves, too—and then I'll just have to leave home."

"I'll warn her, then," Linda said.

Her father laughed. "Don't you dare!"

"Well, I don't want you to leave home. You're always gone. We hardly get to see you, and I'm afraid Amy will forget what you look like."

"Have trouble in remembering yourself?"

"Yes," Linda grinned.

Her father tweaked her ear playfully.

"It's nice to be missed," he said simply. "But I'll try to reform. Can't have my family saying 'Who's that man?' and shutting the door in my face."

Linda had her dishwashing committee all lined up, and plans for the Junior-Senior Feed were practically completed, with everyone breathing in relief and satisfaction, when the blow fell. Christiansen sent word that he couldn't cater for them after all. He was sorry to disappoint; but he had two big weddings that evening, and

216

a reception, and with help so scarce he just couldn't make it.

"What are we going to *do?*" Edith wailed at the meeting which had been hastily called. "It's too late to get anyone else. And, besides, whom could we get?"

"That pretty well ties it, I guess," Buzz Dean said gloomily. "A swell time to throw us over—just four days before the Feed."

"Hasn't anybody got any ideas?" Edith demanded.

Linda stood up. "Yes," she said. "I have."

"Hear, hear!" someone called.

She tried not to discover whether it was admiration or sarcasm. If she got flustered now, it would be too bad.

"I suppose you're going to suggest we give up the whole thing, and then there wouldn't be any dishes to wash," Edith said.

Another nasty crack. But somehow Linda didn't mind. She knew why Edith was that way . . . and it couldn't hurt her.

"On the contrary," she said, as calmly as she could. "I'm going to suggest that we do it all ourselves."

"Ouch!" came in a chorus.

"It wouldn't be hard," Linda said, eagerness coloring her voice now. "I'd be glad to take charge. If you'll tell me just what you have to spend, and let me have the help I need, I'll give you a feed that *is* a feed."

She hoped she didn't sound boastful. Only confident. For she *was* confident. This was right up her alley.

"What makes you think you can do it?" Edith asked,

with an ill-concealed sneer. "It's not just a matter of glory, you know."

"I know," Linda answered quietly. "But I've kept house for years. I know how to buy, and how to plan meals. I'm not afraid of the work, either."

Carol spoke up suddenly, and Linda was grateful for her voice. "I'll say she's a whiz at buying. And she knows some swell menus. Why, she saved my life a couple of months ago. I move we give her a try . . . we've *got* to have the Feed, and if we all pitch in and help— I'm no good at her sort of thing, but I can certainly take orders."

Carol's stand swung the vote Linda's way. They followed meekly where she suggested. Anyhow, Linda thought a little grimly, they were in a jam and she offered a way of escape.

"Well," Edith conceded grumpily, "there isn't much else we can do."

"And that means," Buzz Dean said wickedly, "that—boy!—you'd better be good!"

A laugh ran around the room, but Linda knew there was a good deal of truth in what he said. They weren't so much grateful as desperate. Any port in a storm. She had offered herself and they were going to watch her with eagle-eyed criticism, ready to pounce on her if results didn't come up to expectations.

It was a challenge, yet one that she felt she could meet successfully. Her voice had an authoritative ring.

"Let's get down to details then," she said. And suddenly, looking around at their glum, unbelieving faces, she cried, "Cheer up! This is going to be *fun!*"

218

CHAPTER TWELVE

IT WAS fun. It was hard work, too. Linda had had no delusions about that. The four days that remained were concentrated effort. She bit her pencil over innumerable items. Not everybody liked shrimps. Veal loaf cost too much. Boiled ham would take too long. It was surprising how many ideas had to be eliminated or discarded for one reason or another. These days it wasn't simply a matter of deciding what you'd like to have and then having it. You had to think of rationing, of prices, of markets, of availability. It took some fine juggling to evolve a menu that would be delectable and satisfying, too, and come within the budget. But she had done it.

"We had thin spaghetti with pimiento cream cheese sauce over it," she wrote to Jerrold. "I don't mind telling you what we had, because I know how well fed you are in the Army and I can't make your mouth water. Mounds of spaghetti, pans full of sauce poured over piping hot. Trays and trays of little fresh pork sausage, slowly fried to a crusty brown. Bowls and bowls of cabbage and carrot salad, ground in the chopper, with a dressing that Mother taught me. More bowls of crisp lettuce with orange and grapefruit sections. Small hot rolls. Glasses of hot spiced grapejuice . . . and that wowed them. They had never heard of it, most of them, and they were crazy about it. You see, I neatly got out of the coffee question that way . . . and nobody wanted tea, of course. They drank quarts of it, and called for more."

The auditorium had been transformed. The girls had decked the long tables with gay cloths and low containers of spring flowers. There were place cards done by the talented art students. Everett Gore's orchestra played before the Feed and during it.

"Charming," said Mr. Galbraith, surveying the scene and rubbing his hands. And afterward, *"And* delicious— most unusual in every way. I congratulate you."

Linda, in the cafeteria kitchen, had her forces well marshaled. The spaghetti had been cooked beforehand and the sauce made. Girls were set to making the salads, heating plates, arranging rolls, setting tables. She and a chosen three from the nutrition and cooking class supervised the mixing of the food, and preparation of the sausages; she herself tended to the hot mulled grapejuice. When, at six-thirty, the boys lined up in their rented white coats, to act as waiters, everything was ready. She was proud of her planning, proud of her coordinated efficiency. It was a big task, and so far it had gone smoothly enough.

She took her place with a flushed face and an anxious eye cast over the long tables. The din rose around her, but her mind ignored it. Was there enough celery? Would
220

the boys remember to fill the water glasses? Was the pimiento sauce seasoned enough? . . . Yes, thank goodness, it was. At last she was able to relax a little and let their comments reach her ears.

"Boy, is this good!" . . . "I'm a ravening wolf—I could eat this whole bowl of salad myself." . . . "Brookhaven never had a spread like this in steen years. . . . Have the poor Sophomores got something to strain at!" . . . "Pipe the Seniors, will you? They look like a bunch of Cheshire cats, and ready to burst."

"I always did like that phrase," Buzz Dean rumbled at her left. "The one about being too full for utterance. That's me. It hasn't happened often. And, now that it has, I wonder what a guy is supposed to utter when he isn't too full for utterance?"

"He's supposed to thank the cook," Linda laughed.

"Thank her?" he retorted, with a ludicrous rolling of his eyes. "I'm going to get down on my knees to her . . . when I can budge."

Ben Brixton rose, tapped on his glass for silence. The din subsided to a low mumble.

"There's no need to ask if you enjoyed the Feed," he said. "The tables look as if a hurricane had passed, taking everything with it. I want to thank everybody who was connected with this affair, from the Seniors who deigned to come, down to the lowliest Junior who printed tickets. It wouldn't have been the success it was without your help. But the Feed wouldn't have come off at all if it hadn't been for the noble spirit of Linda Marsh. She

221

rose to the occasion, when disaster threatened, like a true heroine, and she turned what might have been a debacle into a bang-up affair that we can be proud of when we're old men and women. When, as, and if you're able to get up, we're giving her a rising, rousing vote of thanks for what she did."

The tables rose as one man. The orchestra swung into melody, and they roared lustily:

> "For she's a jolly good fellow,
> For she's a jolly good fellow.
> For she's a jolly good fellllloooo . . ."

Crescendos that split the rafters. And then, with a surging downrush:

> "A credit to Brookhaven High!"

When they had finished, Ben said, "Maybe it's not etiquette to tell our guests what we spent to entertain them; but at least they know that we did set aside a sum for that purpose. Linda Marsh took it and worked wonders with it; what's more, she had so much left over that we were able to buy a bunch of war stamps with the savings . . . and this."

From somewhere a Junior approached with a small box, and Linda, quivering with excitement and pleasure, took off the lid and lifted out two white orchids tied with silver ribbon. She stood staring at them.

"Oh!" was all she could say. "Oh!"

"Orchids for Linda!" they cried.

And Linda felt her face crumpling with emotion.

This was surely payment, more than payment enough, for all the work and worry, the heat and hurry, the anxious moments and the aching feet. She had brought success out of threatened failure for them. She had proved herself a valuable member of their group. They had accepted her . . . and called her a jolly good fellow and bought orchids for her.

It was a memorable evening.

They played games after the Feed, and sang songs and put on stunts. One girl did a tap dance, a Junior boy played the accordion so that you couldn't keep your feet still; a solemn-faced lad did magic tricks that left them goggle-eyed; and Everett Gore played a clarinet solo with such real beauty that they were silent a long minute before they broke into applause.

She had started to leave the auditorium in the midst of the program, thinking of the mountain of dishes that must be tackled before she could go home, when Carol whispered, "Sit down! Surprise! . . . Do you think we'd have you doing dishes, *too,* after all the rest? The boys volunteered, and everything's cleared. I don't know how clean they are, but they'll probably pass."

Linda lay awake long that night. She had put the orchids in the refrigerator, jealous of their loveliness. She would hate to see them wither, for they were a kind of symbol to her. Her eyes were wide in the darkness. How nice everybody had been! Really swell! Even Edith Merrick had said grudgingly, "Well, it came off okay, thank

223

heavens!" You couldn't expect much more than that. And Helen Walters hadn't been there, so her mocking smile hadn't spoiled a single moment.

It was too bad Helen couldn't get wise to herself . . . and to others. As *she* had. Praise be, she'd seen the light before it was too late. Little by little it had come to her . . . not like a revelation, in one blinding flash, but as if somebody had opened a door, inch by inch, so that she could glimpse the sunlight in the room beyond and enter.

People weren't antagonistic to you . . . oh, a few perhaps, like Helen and Edith, but they couldn't help being that way. And what of it? You couldn't expect universal approval for everything you did and said. If the people you really liked, liked *you* that was all you could ask. And they couldn't tell whether they liked you or not, could they, until you'd shown them—in some way or other—what you were? By the way you talked, or what you did, or how you acted. They were waiting to judge you . . . not in an unfriendly fashion, but curiously—withholding their friendship until they were sure you were worthy of it, and then, when you had demonstrated your personality, taking you into the circle as naturally as this.

When you realized that, you were able to be yourself. When you realized that, you had an entirely different outlook. Take herself. She had come to Brookhaven, shy, afraid, ready to feel injured and slighted. Lonely. She wanted people to take her in at once, to welcome her into their private little groups which they had built up carefully over months and years. When it didn't happen, she
224

had withdrawn still further into herself. No wonder girls had been indifferent, and boys somewhat appalled. And, besides, what could she *do?* They didn't know . . . they were waiting to see.

It was when she had forgotten herself, when she had risen to put something else above her own personal desires, that she had made them like her. "Orchids for Linda." It was a sweet phrase. And the flowers nestling against the ice tray were a decoration she had won.

News of the Feed spread through the school and, as always, grew in the spreading. Those of the Junior class who hadn't been able to come or who had stayed away because they thought it would be something of a fiasco, were mourning audibly over their hard luck. A member of the Photography Club came to take a snapshot of her for reproduction in the school paper; and there was a nice write-up accompanying it, signed C. B.

Linda found herself being looked at with new interest, asked to join clubs, spoken to by girls who had scarcely known she existed. It was almost funny—all this happening just because she had done something which was in her line but which, apparently, struck others as being a marvelous accomplishment. Of course she heard other comments, too. One from Naomi was typical. "Why *wouldn't* she turn out a good feed with all those girls from the nutrition class helping her? Taking the credit's easy when others do the work." But it didn't touch her. Nothing like that could touch her again.

The days went by with whirlwind pace, at an accelerated tempo that was stimulating and fairly breath-taking. Classwork, afternoons at the Day Nursery, knitting, looking after the house . . . and now plans for the big tea.

The Juniors had been so set up by their success with the Feed that the next step was practically inevitable. Brookhaven was turning all its efforts to preparation for the tremendous Red Cross War Fund Drive. They were determined to go over the top. Several empty stores had been taken as auxiliary recruiting headquarters, volunteer workers were manning them and organizing the soliciting, and Brookhaven High had its own organization for taking contributions.

But Ben Brixton wasn't satisfied. "We've got to have something special," he said. "If we leave it to individuals to give something when, as, and if they feel like it, we'll make a showing, of course, but not the kind that we ought to make. And this isn't an ordinary soliciting. It isn't an ordinary war, either. We've got to make some kind of all-out effort. . . . So what's it to be?" He looked around the room; his eyes lit on Linda. "There's the girl with the bright new set of brains. Give, Linda, give!"

She hadn't had an idea. In fact, she had been sitting back comfortably, thinking that her share had probably been taken care of and it was up to the others to think of something. But under Ben's compelling eye she rose to her feet; from somewhere in her subconscious an idea began to form . . . and before she opened her mouth it was

226

there. Complete. No one could be more astonished than she was, she thought dazedly.

"We might have a tea," she suggested.

She knew they wouldn't think much of that, and they didn't. There were a few moans, and a sort of leaden silence.

"I know you aren't enthusiastic," she went on. "But maybe that's because you don't see it at the moment the way I do. We could use the auditorium. We'd decorate it, so that it would be really beautiful. We'd have tea and coffee, and I know dozens of delectable sandwiches. Nuts; candies; glacéd fruits. Mushroom rolls; toasted cheese delights. Things like that. Various prominent women to pour, in rotation. Everett Gore's orchestra to play tea music. Perhaps the choir to sing at intervals. Special acts put on every hour, but nothing to take over five minutes."

They began to sit up; there was a sparkle of interest in their faces.

"I think you've got something there," Carol said. "I'd love to take charge of the decorating. We could have greens and candles, and masses of forsythia—it's just ready to be forced, and Brookhaven's full of it—and pussy willows. We'd have some wall hangings—I know where I can borrow them—and some lovely old screens. Mrs. Harding's famous tea service, and Mrs. Larew's."

"We'd do it up in businesslike style, too." Ben took her up. "Teams to sell tickets, boys to take care of the advertising . . . the decorating and food preparation to be done by committees."

"With Linda in charge of the food!" more than one voice insisted.

And so it was settled. They would charge fifty cents, they decided.

A number of the class thought that was exorbitant, but Buzz Dean said scornfully, "Not for Linda's food. And not for the War Fund. Why, I'd charge 'em a dollar without turning a hair and tell 'em they were getting a bargain."

"What about the coffee question? And the sugar?" someone asked. "They're rationed, and heaven knows we can't get any from our homes!"

"I think," Ben said slowly, "there's some kind of ruling that if an affair like this is given for charity the Ration Board will let you have supplies. But I'm not sure. Who'll volunteer to see about it?"

"I will," Buzz said promptly. "I'll beard the lions in their den; and if I can't sell them the idea that this is worth giving us special rations for, you can cut me off your list."

A date was set, three weeks ahead. It didn't give them too much time, but they wanted the tea to coincide with the height of the city's drive.

"How about letting the rest of the school in on this?" Jimmy Post asked, in a moment's lull.

"No!" they shouted. "Not on your life!"

228

"If this is to be a success, it's going to be purely a Junior class success. And if it's a fizzle—"

"Perish the thought, you traitor!"

"I was only considering the chances."

"There's nothing but success ahead. Excelsior!"

Ben divided the class into teams. As the days progressed, Linda heard reports. Tickets had been printed gratis by a local firm. Some of the boys had asked boldly for contributions from merchants . . . and the results were so surprising that Linda felt she must pinch herself. Butter, that precious commodity—a quarter pound here, a half pound there. The promise of some cream. Two pounds of salted nuts. All the sandwich bread they needed from the Vienna Bakery. A hundred pots of tulips from the nursery . . . to be returned later. (That sent Carol into rhapsodies and she immediately began planning a new decorative scheme, with all the windows outlined with tulips and a bed of them below the stage.)

The Dainty Shoppe offered candies; the undertaker would send chairs. The Modern Shop would lend furniture to dress up the hall, and lamps and rugs. The list grew, and Linda's own list of things she would have to buy shortened miraculously.

She had selected her menu, and given duties to each girl on her committee. Each knew which sandwich filling she was to prepare; one was put in charge of accessories, another of extras—such as candies and nuts. One was to see about the tea service. The girls who were to serve

229

were notified of the costume they were to wear—white dresses with yellow aprons and yellow ribbons in their hair.

The rest she would look after herself—making certain specialties and getting in the supplies. But that part would have to wait until the last minute, when she knew how many she'd have to prepare for. Buzz Dean came back triumphantly from the Ration Board, saying that he hadn't had any trouble at all and when she knew how much she wanted he would go down and get the necessary permits. Practically everything was taken care of but the matter of choosing which women would pour at which half-hour intervals. Carol's mother, of course, and Mrs. Harding and Mrs. Larew. The Mayor's wife, and Mrs. Galbraith.

"I think it's nice to have Mrs. Heeley, the head of the Red Cross," Linda said. "But couldn't we have Mrs. Wing, too?"

"Good idea!" Carol said. "Will you ask her?"

"Yes, I'll be glad to. And then . . ."

She hesitated. Perhaps it wouldn't do.

But Carol pressed her. "You had somebody else in mind. Who, for goodness' sake? Out with it!"

"I'd like specially to ask Mrs. Clayborne, my neighbor," Linda said.

Mrs. Clayborne wasn't the head of any civic or patriotic committee, but she was important . . . she was important to her. And Linda wanted to honor her in some way.

230

"Why, naturally! That would be swell," Carol concurred. "She's charming. Mother knows her. And if you want her that's settled. That makes eight. Now we can start calling them up and trying to work out who'll pour when!"

Linda skipped through the hedge late that afternoon and rapped on the back door. There was a long silence, and she was just about to enter unbidden when the door opened and Mrs. Clayborne confronted her. Linda was shocked. The gray eyes were tear-filled, the sweet mouth that had smiled comfortingly at her so many times was tight with emotion, and it seemed to Linda that her whole face was thinned with sorrow.

"Is he—is he—gone?" Linda managed at last, fear hammering in her heart.

She remembered in a flash Mrs. Clayborne's premonition. "It may be his last furlough." And Jerrold himself saying soberly, "I may be going far away. Very soon now."

Mary Clayborne said, "No. Not that. I've just had a telegram. He's in the hospital at camp, terribly injured. There was an accident at the field . . . it was his last training flight, and then he was to be sent overseas. Oh, Linda, if only— Comfort me, Linda!"

Linda ran to her and held out her arms. Mrs. Clayborne put her head down on her shoulder, and Linda thought swiftly, "She's the child now, and I'm the mother." She stroked Mrs. Clayborne's hair and made

231

soothing little sounds. And after a while Mary Clayborne lifted her face.

"I had to cry a little, Linda. Now I'll be strong. Jerrold won't want to see a weepy mother."

"Are you going down to him?"

"As soon as I can pack and get a reservation."

"I'll help you pack," Linda offered eagerly. "I'll call the ticket office for you, too, if you'll tell me what you want. I'll look after everything here, Mrs. Clayborne, while you're gone. Oh, I hope you'll find him much better when you get there!"

"I'll stay as long as he's ill, as long as he needs me and I can be near him. I haven't any plans beyond that. I'd thought I'd have to close the house. . . . Oh, Linda, you're so good to me!"

CHAPTER THIRTEEN

SO MRS. CLAYBORNE didn't pour, after all. Linda's last-minute preparations for the tea were overshadowed by the fear and worry that beset her. There had been no news . . . nothing since that anxious moment when her family had seen Mrs. Clayborne off at the station, calling admonitions and messages to take to Jerrold. It overcast her days. It made the war come really close to her. This was the sort of thing that was happening all over the world, in countless homes, to countless friends.

The tea itself was a tremendous success. The committee had sold three hundred tickets.

"That means," Linda said, "that I'll have to prepare for four hundred—there'll be plenty of payers-at-the-door."

She checked over lists, helpers, supplies. And four hundred and fifty came.

When she reached home that night, scarcely able to drag one foot after the other, she flung herself into a deep chair. She could still hear the frightful buzz that bespoke a successful party. The clank of dishes and spoons. The strains of Everett Gore's orchestra. She could close her lids and see piles of dishes rising to the ceiling, plates of sandwiches appearing and disappearing like some act of magic; smell the scent of fresh-made coffee every half-hour, the mingled perfumes of the women, the fragrance of spring flowers wilting in the heat.

Oh, it had been a success all right. Hardly a salted nut left. Not a single sandwich. Dregs of tea. But no one had gone without his share, and her ears hummed with the compliments that she had heard. It had gone off with a bang. And the Junior class had one hundred and eighty dollars to turn over to the American Red Cross, Brookhaven Chapter. If that wasn't a feather in their cap, she didn't know a feather when she saw one.

She expelled a deep breath. The telephone rang. "Mrs. Parsons," she called wearily, "you take it, please. If it's the police, tell them I'm sorry—I'll never do it again. If a nut is missing, tell them I'll find it in the morning. If somebody broke a dish, I don't care. I'm going to take a hot bath and lie down; and don't call me, no matter what!"

Mrs. Parsons, one hand on the telephone, said severely, "You'll drink a glass of hot milk, just the same, before you turn in. Seems to me you need it . . . you almost sound delirious to me."

Linda laughed. "Just deliriously happy that it turned out so well, and if I have fallen arches it's all in a good cause and I won't complain."

234

She ran upstairs, closed her door, and flung herself on the bed. Heavens, it felt good to relax! With arms outspread she lay staring at the ceiling. If she closed her eyes a moment she'd see dishes and spoons again, and crowds of people. It was pleasant to think it was all over, *and* a success. One hundred and eighty dollars! They'd rate a special letter of thanks from the Board of Directors for that.

Suddenly she was aware of strange yappings and growls that came from Amy's room and that had been going on ever since she came up.

"Amy!" she called. "What in the world are you doing? It sounds as if you're torturing poor Jinks."

The yappings ceased and Amy's pointed little face appeared at the door, cautiously opened a trifle.

"I was just— What's the matter? Are you sick?"

Linda laughed. "No, I'm sorry to disappoint you. I know you want to try out some new canine medicine on me; but I'm not having any, thanks. I'm just dog-weary. What do you do for Jinks when he's dog-weary?"

Amy said soberly, "He never gets that way. I don't let him work too hard, or play too hard either. And I give him the right food."

"Well, you're no help," Linda said indulgently. "Only tell me, what was going on in there? It sounded distressing."

"I'm teaching Jinks a new trick. Not a new *trick* exactly . . . he's got to learn something so he can do some

235

good. He doesn't want to learn today. But he *can*," she hastened to add. "He's so full of personality it's awfully hard to teach him . . . sometimes."

"What's he supposed to learn?"

"Well"—Amy perched tentatively on the side of the bed—"I couldn't give him for an Army dog, you know, and I was glad. But I didn't feel just right about it, either. So I thought he and I ought to do something for Dogs for Defense. And I thought and thought. Now I've got it. I'm going to teach him to hold a little basket in his mouth, and I'm going to make him a placard to wear around his neck; and we'll stand on the corner downtown some place where there are lots of people, and people will drop pennies, or nickels maybe, in the basket and we'll send them to the fund for Dogs for Defense." Her face lit up. "Don't you think that's a grand idea?"

Linda was careful to keep her face straight.

"Grand," she agreed. "But don't you think it would be best to ask first if that's the sort of thing you may do? You know, the Mayor might have other ideas. Or some organization might be putting on a campaign and not want you working separately. . . . Why, you'd practically steal the show with Jinks holding a basket!"

Amy considered this.

"Maybe I'd better," she said. "I never thought of that. I just knew they wanted money and this would be a quick way to get it—and cute, too. *Everybody'd* love Jinks; they couldn't help putting something in his basket."

236

"Of course," Linda said warmly. "Only it's wise to be sure of your ground first."

"I'll go down and see the Mayor tomorrow," Amy decided, getting up with a purposeful air.

"No, wait," Linda said hurriedly.

How could she stop Amy?

"Why? If you have to see the Mayor, you have to see him. I don't mind. He looks like a nice man from his pictures. I'll take Jinks along. The Mayor might not care to do it if I just told him about it; but, seeing Jinks, he'll have to agree."

"Perhaps you're right," Linda said in a weak voice. She felt incapable of arguing. When Amy made up her mind, there was little you could do about it. And she might succeed, at that. Still, she ought to make one more effort. "The Mayor's very busy these days, Amy."

"I know. But this is important. I'll just wait if I have to."

Linda rolled over and smothered something between a laugh and a sigh in her pillow. Then she got up . . . she wasn't quite so tired now.

When she came down, after a hot bath and a rub, Mrs. Parsons said, "That was Western Union on the phone. I wrote down what they said."

Linda took the sheet with Mrs. Parsons' cramped handwriting; her fingers shook as she scanned it. "Jerrold will get well. So happy. Both legs in casts, very tedious. Am staying. Letter follows. Love to all. Mary Clayborne."

237

"Now that's what I call good news," Mrs. Parsons said. "My, I felt so sorry for her—all alone like that, and then her son took with an accident. I miss her around. She's a real lady."

"I miss her, too," Linda said.

She missed her friend more than she could say. She had gone over daily, dusted a little, watered the plants, aired the rooms. The house seemed to speak to her, eloquent of its absent mistress; and she had thought how much personality a house could have, because of its occupants. Would their house, if they moved away, speak to someone who came in as charmingly as Mary Clayborne's did, or hadn't they lived there long enough? Houses took on color and life from their owners, that was sure. All the happy days, even the little worries; the meals you had had, the laughter, the open fires, the quiet evenings, built up an atmosphere as tangible as a picture. Long after people had left, something of that atmosphere lingered in the rooms.

"Let's make Jerrold a book," Linda said suddenly one evening at supper, after she had read them Mrs. Clayborne's letter telling about the long wearisome hours Jerrold had to spend staring at the ceiling or counting slats in the blinds.

"A book!" Amy and Bob chorused, and Amy said, "But who writes?"

"Not that kind of book," Linda explained. "A sort of scrapbook. Cartoons, and verses; jokes . . . anything that looks interesting or would make him smile."

238

"I get you!" Bob cried. "I saw a swell cartoon in the *Post* yesterday. I'll cut it out."

"There were some awfully cute pictures of a dog doing tricks in our school paper," Amy offered with eagerness. "I could make a page of those and then, maybe, tell him what Jinks can do, and put in the snap I took of him with the biscuit on his nose."

Linda nodded. "That's just what I mean. I have an idea, too."

She didn't tell them what it was; but she took the next afternoon off and telephoned the various friends of Jerrold whom she had met at his party, and asked each of them to write a letter to him—as gay and humorous as they could make it, and full of news that they knew he'd like to hear. She would call for it, she said, and paste it in the book she was making to send him.

She met with surprising success. Writing to Jerrold, well and vigorous and busy, was one thing . . . a thing they kept putting off. But writing to a Jerrold confined to his cot in casts, and bandaged and bored, was quite another. They'd all do it, they said, and gladly, and she was clever to think of the idea.

She bought colored cardboards at the stationer's, cut them to size, punched holes in the margin, and tied them together with lacing. Bob hand-lettered the pages; and she cut out decorations and pasted them on each one, making them as varied as possible. She alternated the letters from his friends with pages of verse, humorous squibs, and the other material she had collected; and at the last minute she went the rounds again and asked for small, informal photographs of his friends, and made a section of those. The pages were pasted together then on the edges, and each was labeled with a date: "To be opened Sunday, March sixth," "To be read Tuesday, March eighth," "Don't open until Thursday, March tenth," and so on . . . enough for six weeks of tedium. Something, she hoped, that he would have to look forward to every other day for a month and a half. By that time he wouldn't need a book like this to occupy his mind or give him a moment's respite. In between, she told him in the accompanying note, she would badger him with letters.

"But," she ended, "it seems to me the tables have been turned somehow. You told me to keep an eye on your mother, and I've tried to do it. Only now she has had to go and keep an eye on you. And it's all wrong."

Linda had forgotten about Amy and her Dogs for Defense project, but Amy had not. On the day the book to Jerrold was sent off, express prepaid, Amy burst in with her news.

"I did it! I saw him! And what do you think he said?"

"Did what? Saw whom?"

"The Mayor, of course," Amy said impatiently. "I went the other day; but he was all tied up, his sec-etary said, with conferences, but she put me down for today at three-thirty. And today I went, with Jinks, and he saw me. I sat in a great big chair by his desk, near the window, and Jinks was right beside me. I told Jinks to give the
240

Mayor a paw; and he did, right off. And then I told him what I was there for, and he listened—oh, very politely —and when I finished he said, 'Young lady, you've got something there. But I have an idea, too. Don't you think the Dogs for Defense campaign could wait till we're through with the War Fund drive?' And I said, 'Well, of course, if you think it would be better. I don't want to interfere or anything.' And he laughed, and said Jinks and I were something of a menace at that. I didn't get what he meant, but that's what he said. So he went on and asked me what I thought of *his* idea, and that was that I could take Jinks, just like I said, down to a corner with his basket—only the placard ought to read, 'Give to the American Red Cross War Fund, please!'"

"Well!" Linda said, in real amazement. She could see that Amy was expecting her to say something, but that was all she could think of. Amy had done it! "Well!" she repeated.

"I knew it would be easy," Amy said complacently. "With Jinks along. We'll do the Red Cross first; then maybe we can do Dogs for Defense. The Mayor said he'll call the proper 'thorities, and let me know what day I'm to go downtown and where I'm to be—but only if it's nice weather, he said. I told him Jinks and I didn't care about the weather. . . . I have a raincoat, and Jinks has such a good natural coat he doesn't need any. And we weren't softies, I told him. But he said he heard I'd almost got pneumonia and he wouldn't be responsible and, anyhow, more people came out on a fine day."

241

Linda said, "Amy, I think you'll get wherever you're going."

Amy answered promptly, "I'm going to be a vet'-narian."

"A veterinarian, dear," Linda corrected patiently. "If you're going to be one, you ought to learn to say it correctly."

"Yes," Amy agreed, but her mind was patently elsewhere. "Anyhow, everybody just says 'vet.' I'm going to have a sign out on my house, 'Amy Marsh, Vet . . . Dogs and Cats.' I don't think I'd like to work with horses and cows."

"I'm surprised you include cats." Linda laughed. "I thought perhaps you'd confine yourself to dogs, and wire-haired terriers at that."

"Telephone, Miss Linda," Mrs. Parsons interrupted.

It was Carol Burroughs.

"May I come over, Lin?" she asked in excitement. "I've something to take up with you. I just had a call from Mrs. Larew, and you can't imagine what she wants! It's sort of haywire, but wait till you hear it! Maybe we could do it at that."

"Hurry up," Linda ordered. "It's not fair to tantalize people over the phone."

Carol dismounted from her bicycle ten minutes later.

"I didn't even stop to leave word where I was going," she said, "so I'll have to be getting back in a rush."

"Not till you sit down and tell me what all this is about. I'm as curious as—as Jinks with a new scent."

"It'll mean work," Carol warned.

"What doesn't these days?" Linda retorted. "What kind of work?"

"Well, more or less the kind we've been doing. . . . Only different."

"So explicit!" Linda scoffed. She seized a heavy book and made a menacing gesture. "Come across now, Carol, or else—"

Carol laughed. "Well, I can see you're pining for it, so here goes. Mrs. Larew was so impressed with our handling of the tea that she got an idea. It practically took her breath away, I gather, and she debated it for days with herself. She would have called you directly, but it seems you made such an impression on her that she was afraid to approach you. So I'm a sort of intermediary. I'm to lay this before you in its best dress, and see if you'll consent to handle it . . . with the help of the rest of us."

"Yes, yes?" Linda said on an impatient rising inflection, book still poised.

"Have a heart! I'm getting to the point as fast as I can. . . . She's entertaining the Kings' Daughters next week. Not just her circle, but the whole Brookhaven organization. At a tea. She's head of it, you know, and she has a lovely old house. Well, it seems the usual procedure has always been to have some of the women do the work; each year they were supposed to rotate, she said; but it turned out that certain women were such good workers they were always on the committees. This time

243

she wants to give the faithful ones a complete rest and change. She said they shouldn't have to do a thing, as a reward for virtue. She hasn't the servants to handle it alone, so she thought we might take over. She'd pay us what she would have to pay a caterer or extra help, and we could use the money whichever way we pleased . . . probably, she thought, for our favorite war work."

"Which would be the Red Cross," Linda supplemented.

Carol said, "That goes without saying. I liked the idea, myself. I don't see why we couldn't do it, but of course it would be up to you. You're the guiding star and presiding genius and the brains behind the brawn and all that."

"Of course," Linda said, with an exaggerated smirk. "So nice to be appreciated."

"Well, you are. We know it, and so does Mrs. Larew. She said of course you'd have to be in charge; and I said, 'But of course!' After that she breathed easier. . . . What do you say?"

"I say I'll have to have a minute to think it over. But, offhand, why not? It would be fun to earn some extra money for the Red Cross, and we could do it. Would the others be willing to help, do you think?"

"I know they would. I'll take care of corralling the help, if you'll preside over the organizing," Carol offered. "Mrs. Larew is quite set up with the thought of doing something different, and she said, 'It would be lovely to have young girls serving for a change, instead of elderly maids or tottery men in badly fitting coats. Quite in keeping with spring, and all that.' I felt like saying, 'Tra-la'
244

or 'Tweet-tweet' or something equally in keeping, but fortunately I didn't."

"Fortunately." Linda leaned her head on her hands and thought. "How much time would we have?" she looked up to ask.

"She's issuing invitations for two weeks from to-morrow."

"That would be enough time. What about the menu?"

"She said she'd leave it to you, and get in whatever you ordered; or she'd plan one herself and also see to the supplies, whichever you preferred. She just wants us to make the stuff and see to the serving and clearing up afterward, and she said she'd give us twenty-five dollars for that."

"Sold!" Linda jumped up. "Tell her it's a date. . . . Does she want it in writing?"

Carol grabbed her by the hand. "Oh, Lin, I'm so re-lieved! I wouldn't have blamed you for a minute for turning it down, because it does mean a lot of work and responsibility; but I'm so glad you're willing to take it on. The Junior class will make a name for itself yet . . . as well as all this extra cash for a good cause. I think you're swell to do it."

"Not to mention how grand it is to have help like you and Dana and Sue and the rest."

"Put on your coat and let's go and see Mrs. Larew right away, before she reneges in favor of the elderly maids. Do you think she'd like some music, too? Perhaps we could work Everett in."

245

"Talk it up. She seems ripe for anything. . . . Do you know, Carol," she called, searching in the closet for her jacket, "I have the queerest feeling. As if this were the beginning of something."

"It's the beginning of some more headaches for you and the amassing of twenty-five dollars for us, anyhow."

"No," said Linda slowly, "that isn't what I mean. But I don't know exactly what I *do* mean." She shook herself. "Well, come on, let's go."

CHAPTER FOURTEEN

IT *WAS* the beginning—the beginning of a whole new undertaking, although it wasn't until two weeks after the Larew tea that the queer feeling Linda had had blossomed into an inspiration. Even so, it might never have reached the practical stage if it hadn't been for Mrs. Wing and the fact that her cook walked out on her at the last minute when her husband was bringing home four men to dinner.

"And that settled it," Linda wrote to Mrs. Clayborne. Her pen raced over the page in her impatience to put down all the circumstances that had contributed to this particular moment. "She called me up about five o'clock in sheer desperation. Christiansen was out of the question; Clara Peters, the colored woman who caters and serves, couldn't be reached; the Club couldn't take any more reservations, and she was frantic. It seems, anyhow, that her husband had told her he had promised these men—who'd been living in Washington hotels— a good home-cooked dinner! She asked if I could possibly come and take charge, and bring along one or two others. All the food was there, or she'd get anything I said. Well, to make a long story short, I called Carol and

Buzz Dean, and we went over and tackled the situation. It was really fun! Buzz served, and he was perfect. Carol helped prepare things, I did the cooking, and we all cleaned up afterward. Mrs. Wing was so grateful she practically wept on our necks, and gave us ten dollars for our services. We turned it back to her at once for the Red Cross fund, and right there the idea was born."

Linda had waited until they were trudging home, somewhat weary but highly satisfied.

"Mrs. Wing's our friend for life," she said, smiling to herself in the dark.

"And—boy!—did Mr. Wing's rating go up with those men! They almost licked the platters. . . . You're some cook, Linda," Buzz said warmly.

"Thanks. You're not half bad yourselves. . . . You know, I was thinking that we could do this regularly."

Buzz and Carol stopped in their tracks. She could not see their faces, but their voices were incredulous and surprised.

"You mean—" Carol managed at last. "You mean go to peoples' homes and serve dinner?"

"Not that exactly. But this town hasn't a decent place to eat outside of the Club. And the caterers are few and far between and getting more independent every day. If people want to eat out, where can they go—now that gas rationing's so strict? The answer is 'Nowhere.' And that's our chance."

"I don't get it," Buzz complained. "Come clean, Linda."

248

"Well, what I mean is we could band together and serve dinners. It would be open to the public—it would have to be, because that's the only way we could get rationed supplies—but we'd have to have reservations. Nobody served without a reservation. That way we'd know exactly how many we had to cater for."

"Good grief!" Buzz exploded. "What are you trying to do—run in competition with the Waldorf or something?"

"Oh heavens, no! We'd be small and exclusive. Just a dozen or so. It would all depend."

"I'll say it would depend!" Carol echoed. "It's a breath-taking scheme. But how in the world—"

"I know," Linda said patiently. "I haven't figured out all the details yet. It just hit me between the eyes tonight, but I thought I'd share it with you and see how you felt."

"We'd do it as our contribution to the Red Cross, of course?" Carol said.

"Of course. That's the main reason. It's a field that is wide open to us—I know we wouldn't have any trouble getting people to patronize us—and it's something we can do. We proved that with the class supper and the teas and now this dinner. I think it would be fun, and good experience, and a money-maker besides."

"Oh, it would be swell!" Carol said enthusiastically. "But *where* would we have it, for one thing? We can't rent a store; it would cost too much and, anyway, there wouldn't be the proper facilities—"

"No, I'd thought of someone's home."

"But no one would want to give over his home like that every night."

"Not every night. Say just two nights a week. Thursdays, when the maids—such as they are—are out; and Sundays, when we could serve a special supper."

"Even so, Lin, it's practically impossible. We could take turns, of course, each of us having it in his home once or twice, if our mothers consented; but it would make for a lot of confusion, and people would have to know where they were going. And at the last minute something might happen—one of the children have measles or something like that—in the house where the dinner was to be held. And then what?"

"And that's where we are now," Linda wrote to Mrs. Clayborne. "Stymied. I refuse to have my project blown to bits by present-day conditions, but for the life of me I don't see a way out. I had everything else so beautifully planned, too. We were going to keep it quite simple; just have one menu, you know, like a family. I was going to call them Potluck Dinners. The sort of thing you'd get if you dropped in on a family. Like it or lump it! And generally you like it, particularly if it's well thought out and well cooked, as our dinners would be. I know people would love the chance to eat out, with home cooking and in a home atmosphere. . . . If only we could solve our problem of finding a place to do it!"

Mary Clayborne's answering telegram was in Linda's hands before she believed her letter had reached her neighbor. "No problem at all. Use my house and all that's in it. Think you have stunning idea there. May I help when I come home?"

Linda could scarcely believe her good fortune. And yet, she thought, staring down at the bit of yellow paper in her hand, hadn't she perhaps had Mary Clayborne's house in mind all along when she talked about "home atmosphere"? When she had told Carol and Buzz that they could serve twelve or fifteen, hadn't she been thinking of the size of Mrs. Clayborne's dining room? Her subconscious must have been at work, although when she wrote she hadn't been aware of it. But Mrs. Clayborne was a darling; she was an *angel,* to have read between the lines and come across with her generous offer so promptly.

Linda flew to the phone and summoned Carol. "We're all set. Fools' luck or potluck, it's *luck* all right. We've got to make a go of it now."

Together they made a list of people to notify, and concocted a placard to set up in the Red Cross rooms downtown. "Have You Tried Potluck Dinners at Clayborne House? Delicious cooking . . . charming atmosphere. Thursdays at 6:30—Sundays at 7. $1.25, no tipping, and all proceeds for the benefit of the American Red Cross. For reservations telephone Brookhaven 399 by six o'clock of the previous day." That was Linda's number. Mrs. Parsons had promised to take all calls carefully, putting down the names on a pad.

As her contribution to the success of the enterprise,

251

too, she volunteered to go over and give Mrs. Clayborne's house a thorough cleaning.

"Oh, I know you've aired and dusted it a little," she said, when Linda protested, "but a good turning out is what it needs, and I'll see that it has it."

It was shining and fresh when the first Thursday came. Linda had gone over early and pushed up the thermostat, and just before the first guests were due she lit a fire on the living room hearth. The refectory table gleamed with a satin sheen; the place mats were precisely set; the glassware sparkled; the silver shone. Plates were warming in the oven; salads were chilling in the refrigerator. Color flew high in Linda's cheeks as she surveyed the dining room. Eight places at the main table; a small table for four in the bay window. Candles in glass holders . . . jonquils in low bowls. Folded napkins; butter pats. Everything was there.

She hoped the guests came promptly. So much depended on this first dinner; if it was a success, news of it would spread by word of mouth—which was the best advertising in the world. And this had to be a success! It was her own project, of course, but the entire Junior class had an interest in it; twelve of them were actively taking part in it. There were to be three different members, beside herself, in the kitchen each night. Girls to prepare salads and desserts, boys to help with the vegetables and do the serving. A dishwashing team, and a clearing-up team. They reported at four and expected to be free at eight, but had promised to stay as long as necessary. She could hear the subdued chatter of Ben, Carol, and Buzz in the kitchen now. They were as excited as she. . . . Oh, how could they be? This was her brain child. *Nobody* could feel quite the way she did about it.

The door chimes sounded. Linda darted toward the kitchen as Ben went forward, in his white coat, to answer. His red hair gleamed in the light.

"Welcome to Clayborne House!" she heard him say.

For the tenth time she went over the list of guests, because she liked the sound. Carol's parents, and the Brixtons. Mr. and Mrs. Galbraith. The Larews, the Wings, and Mr. and Mrs. Heeley.

"Aren't we coming?" Bob had demanded, scowling. "Gosh, that's a nice way to treat your own family!"

"You can come some night when the reservations fall off," Linda grinned. "And it'll cost you a dollar twenty-five just like all the rest."

"I guess we can stand it at that," Mr. Marsh said. "It's pleasant to eat out, if only next door."

"Well, I think it's queer we can't get in tonight." Bob was disappointed and showed it.

"Even the Mayor and his wife were too late," Linda consoled him. "Cheer up . . . the night you come I'll make chocolate pudding."

Buzz, wrapped in a big apron, was sharpening the carving knife and making what he claimed were cheflike sounds.

"Bring on the roast!" he cried. "And I'll hack it to bits."

253

Linda lifted the roast from the pan to the big platter.

"Nice thin slices," she cautioned, "and even. But not *too* thin. If you don't do this right, Buzz, you don't eat. It's up to you."

"Gosh, those peanut sweet-potato patties smell good," Ben sniffed. "If I don't snatch a couple off somebody's plate it'll be because I have herculean self-control."

"A fine sight it would be," Carol scoffed, "to have the class president snitching food from hungry guests who had *paid* for their meals."

"The tossed salad is what I *ought* to go for," Buzz said, testing the blade along his thumb, "but I intend to fill up on lemon chiffon pie."

"If there's any left," Linda warned. "The kitchen staff get only the crumbs, don't forget."

Turning out the peas, stirring flour into the gravy, giving a last toss to the greens, Linda felt sudden tears in her eyes. If her mother could see her now! All those long years of training were having their effect; all those careful reiterations, those gentle, but firm, reminders, were culminating for Linda in this. . . . "Don't cover the peas, so they'll stay green. . . . Just enough flour to keep it from being thin. . . . Add the milk *slowly,* dear. . . . Crisp your lettuce beforehand. . . . Wash up as you go along and there won't be a mountain of pans to scare you later."

She could hear that beloved voice; she could see herself, a small girl with eager hands and wide eyes, laboriously twirling the beater, measuring out coffee, putting away groceries. She had only been intent on pleasing her mother, on learning how to do things so that she could help. She had never dreamed it would turn into something like this—a talent that stood her in good stead, that made her family happy and well fed and left her classmates goggle-eyed.

"Lin, you're a wizard!" Carol exclaimed. "Everything done on the minute; the kitchen practically as neat as when we started. Hot things hot and cold things cold. . . . And everything so *good!*"

"Oh, you've been sampling, have you?" Buzz said belligerently. "Only crumbs for the kitchen help, Lin said, but apparently you're taking yours beforehand."

Ben and Buzz came back from their serving trips with heart-warming reports. "Mrs. Wing wants the recipe for these patties." . . . "Mr. Galbraith said he never eats salad, but he ate this and why the devil—yep, that's what he said—why the devil can't his wife find a salad dressing like yours?" . . . "Dad asked why in the world I couldn't have warned him there was going to be a super-duper pie so he could have saved some room!"

"No waste here," Carol commented, scraping plates which were already fairly well scraped.

"All gone to the waist," Buzz muttered.

"Any more like that," Ben threatened, "and you don't even get the crumbs."

"The smells have gone to my head, I guess." Buzz grinned, unrepentant. "When do we *eat?*"

Linda had to go and take a bow from the enthusiastic guests.

255

"Just like in novels, my dear," Carol murmured excitedly. "Royalty calling for the chef, you know, and decorating him—her. Hurry up. Your hair looks fine, and there isn't a spot on your apron."

They complimented her extravagantly, and promised to tell all their friends.

"Except," said Mrs. Wing dolefully, "that, if we're generous and tell all our friends, there will probably never be room for us any more!"

Ben came out to the kitchen with a fistful of bills and change. "Not a grumble when they paid. In fact, they acted as if it was a privilege."

"I've kept exact account of everything," Linda said, reaching over to the cabinet for a little book, "and so now I can write down—profits, $5.39. Not bad, is it?"

"I don't like that thirty-nine cents. Sounds pikerish." Buzz reached in his pocket, and brought out a penny. "Contribution. Make it five-forty, just for my sake," he begged.

There was no doubt, after that first evening, that Pot-luck Dinners could continue. The very next morning Mrs. Parsons reported three reservations for Sunday night supper, and by Friday evening they had sixteen and were regretfully compelled to disappoint four others. Linda spent her spare minutes making up menus, reading food advertisements and cookery columns, keeping an eye on grocery prices and what was fresh or abundant in the markets. She enjoyed making up menus—it was chiefly a matter of arranging them so that she could take advantage of what was available or what was reasonable at the moment.

All the dishes her mother had taught her and that she had made for years came to her service now. Pancakes and sausages . . . roast chicken . . . cheese soufflé . . . candied carrots . . . deep-dish rhubarb pie . . . vegetable chowder . . . floating islands . . . casserole of eggs and mushrooms . . . spinach ring and Mexican rice—she knew a sense of elation, a deep satisfaction, in preparing these things that were so tempting and so nourishing. People exclaimed over them and asked for the recipes. The things that sent them away well fed and brought them back again. The dishes that were building up a reputation for her, and a nice bank account for the Junior class to hand to the Red Cross.

Oh, there were bad moments occasionally, and a near fiasco or two. The time the electricity went off, just at six, and there was no current for the stove and they had to finish cooking dinner at the Marshes', rushing things back and forth in covered dishes. The time Ben slipped and broke four glasses. The time Linda was talking over her shoulder and poured the white sauce down the sink. . . . They could laugh about them afterward, but at the moment they were near tragedies. Mrs. Cummings losing her glasses and Mr. Hapgood gallantly searching for them, crying triumphantly, "Here they are!" and then stepping on them! . . . Small Eddie Jenkins howling that his milk was too warm and refusing to eat his carrots. . . . The night the refrigerator didn't function and the ice cream melted. But Linda had fixed *that*. "Quick, Ben, bike down to the Vienna Bakery and get two sponge cakes to slice, and I'll pour this as a sauce over the slices!"

Linda submitted her menus to Miss Pound, the domestic science instructor, and felt as if she'd been given a medal when Miss Pound found nothing to criticize, and much to praise. Moreover, she asked, as a special favor, if Linda could work in various girls from her classes . . . she would like to announce that they would get extra credit that way. "Besides a lot of valuable experience," she added with a smile.

So their reputation grew, and the fund in the bank . . . and suddenly, without a word of warning, Mrs. Clayborne came home.

She came one evening when the Marshes were having an early dinner so that they could go to the first show at the movies. She must have silenced Mrs. Parsons and slipped into the dining room doorway while they were talking, for all at once they looked up and there she was.

Mr. Marsh leaped up.

"Mary!" he cried. Linda was struck by his voice. And how long had he called Mrs. Clayborne "Mary"? She had never noticed it before; but now she could not help but see the eager light in his eyes, and his voice had a special welcome in it. "When did you drive up? We didn't hear you."

"I haven't been in my house yet," she said, smiling at all of them. "I left my bags on the front steps and came right over when I saw your lights. How I've missed you!"

258

"Jerrold, how's Jerrold?" they chorused.

"Almost well, of course, or I shouldn't be here. He's walking with crutches now, and the doctor promises a cane next week. Oh, my dears, he'll walk again as well as ever—I have the doctor's word for it! And I know he's better, because he's frightfully cross! It was lovely to hear him practically bite my head off, because I knew he was well enough to be impatient. . . . So I *had* to come home."

"And what a blessing *that* is," Mr. Marsh said on a deep note.

She had to hear all about Potluck Dinners. "Of course you wrote me about them—I read the letters to Jerrold and he fairly drooled over some of those menus—but I want to hear all about it by word of mouth. With gestures!"

Linda obliged, sketching in as rapidly as possible the phenomenal success of Clayborne House.

"You mustn't give it up," Mrs. Clayborne said. "One of the reasons I came home was that I was envious, and I felt I had to have a hand in it. Would you let me peel vegetables? I'm very experienced, ma'am . . . and I can furnish good references."

"You can do anything you like, even boss us," Linda said fondly. "But I don't know how long we'll be able to keep up, with the new rationing. It makes things pretty difficult and the portions have to be smaller, and all kinds of restrictions are creeping up on us . . . but I won't succumb without a struggle."

Anyhow, she thought happily, Potluck Dinners had served their purpose. They had made money for the cause; they had welded a group of them together in a common effort; they had made a sure place for her and given her the kind of confidence she had never had before.

"And what about the chemistry shack?" Mrs. Clayborne was asking. "I seem to have heard very little about it lately."

Bob thrust his hands in his pockets.

"Aw, well," he said, his face getting red, "I guess I've got plenty of time to be a chemist. Later, maybe. Right now I'm busy getting the place ready for a Victory garden. I'm going to grow all our vegetables—and all the stuff Linda needs, too."

"He just sprang it on us yesterday," Linda said. "He told me he was going to sell us the vegetables, but I'm trying to persuade him to let his better nature have the upper hand and give them to us free. He might as well be truly patriotic while he's about it!"

"Speaking of gardens," Mr. Marsh said, "come out and look at the spring miracles, Mary. I've a lot to show you."

"Aren't we going to the movies?" Amy demanded, gazing after them.

"There's always the second show," Linda reminded her. "Tonight's a special night."

"Well," Amy sighed, "I'll go and give Jinks a walk, then."

Linda, with a queer, excited, nameless feeling helped

Mrs. Parsons clear the table. As she blew out the candles there was a quick ring at the door.

"I'll go," she said.

And there stood Ben.

"I know it's early, but I'm an emissary," he told her, stepping inside. "Mother wants to know if you can come to dinner tomorrow. She's been wanting to have you for a long time; but it's taken her all this while to get her courage up, after tasting your cooking!"

"Silly!" Linda laughed. "Not your mother . . . I mean you. You're making it up."

"No, cross my heart and hope to die. Mother's a good cook in her own right—I'll vouch for that—but she's got an inferiority complex. She says if you can be that good when you're so young she should be much better at her age. . . . And I can tell you now that it's *not* going to be potluck at our house tomorrow night."

"I'd love to come," Linda said warmly. The excited feeling grew.

"D'you know," Ben offered, draping himself over one end of the couch, "that potluck idea of yours was a brain storm. The climax to a whole series of brain storms." He cocked his head and looked at her admiringly. "You're a pretty bright girl, Linda. . . . I've been interested in you for a long time."

"Really?" she grinned. "Who would have thought it?"

"I know I'm slow," he said without apology. "But I'm the slow kind that's sure, too."

"What are you sure of now?"

"That you're the girl I want to take to the Junior Hop," he brought out promptly.

Linda caught her breath. The Junior Hop! The Junior Hop with Ben! She had dreamed of all kinds of things, but she hadn't quite dared to dream of this.

" 'A credit to Brookhaven High,' " Ben was humming.

"Brookhaven's done a lot for *me*," Linda said, suddenly grateful.

She was seeing, in a series of quick illuminating flashes, how far she had come from those first unhappy days when she was lonely, diffident, and reserved . . . holding herself aloof and yet wondering why she was not welcomed into the circles where she longed to be.

So much had happened in those nine months. Looking back, it seemed almost like a lifetime. Because, in a way, it was a whole new life that had developed. She had found herself through a series of slow, painful experiences. She had proved herself, to her own satisfaction and others'. She was where she wanted to be now—part of the circle, busy, important, happy in companionship and service. That, at least, wasn't luck. She had brought it about by her own effort. She was, in a sense, she thought, a sort of self-made girl . . . and the kind of girl she had always wanted to be. She looked ahead now with eagerness. Life held all kinds of interesting possibilities. She might keep up with Potluck Dinners . . . she might go to college (she ought to tell Mr. Galbraith that; he would be pleased) . . . she might specialize in domestic science or dietetics; teach, or open her own tearoom. . . .

"Yes," she repeated, "Brookhaven's done a lot for me."

"Not to mention what you've done for Brookhaven," Ben said stoutly. "You going to be here this summer?"

"It looks like it."

"So are we. . . . Well, I might as well warn you that I'll be cluttering up your doorstep. I'm going to get a defense job, of course; but, even so, you'll probably fall over me every time you go out."

She laughed. "It doesn't frighten me at all."

"By the way," Ben said, "where's your father?"

"Mrs. Clayborne came home. They're in the garden," Linda answered.

Her gaze flew to the window. Twilight had deepened, but she could see her father and Mary Clayborne walking up the path. They stopped then, and there was something about the way they looked at each other . . . Oh, if *that* should happen, too, her cup of happiness would be full.